The
GHOST
of the
KENAI

AURORA HARDY

Epicenter Press Inc.
Alaska Book Adventures™

KENMORE, WA

6524 NE 181st St., Suite 2, Kenmore, WA 98028

Epicenter Press is a regional press publishing nonfiction
books about the arts, history, environment, and diverse
cultures and lifestyles of Alaska and the Pacific Northwest.
For more information, visit www.EpicenterPress.com

The Ghost of the Kenai
Copyright © 2025 by Aurora Hardy

Cover design: Scott Book
Interior design: Melissa Vail Coffman

Library of Congress Control Number: 2024940169

ISBN: 978-1-684922-26-0 (Trade Paperback)
ISBN: 978-1-684922-27-7 (Ebook)

To my children and grandchildren
Memory of Father Juvenal

Not written to portray the past
A glance back and nothing more
Visions of dreams and fantasy
While walking the sandy shore
—Aurora Hardy

ONE

ANCESTORS, ACCEPT MY GIFT. Look upon me kindly and bless my hunting. I am Qadanalchen, son of the Qeshqa, Chief of the Denaina. Qadanalchen, also known as Acts Quickly, laid the offering of dried fish on the ground. He stood in a little clearing with his cousins, Spear and Last Waters. The sparse meadow was held in reverence by the Denaina as a burial ground of a village from the earliest memory. Gifts of food were left for the ancestors before hunting or fishing or berry picking activities began. The ancients smiled on the gifts and blessed the givers with abundance. The birch and alder leaves on the trees at the edges of the opening were yellowing. The promise of the sun rising over the Chugach Mountains began to sear the skies.

The three young men stood in silence, like the sturdy birch trees that walled the meadow. Acts Quickly murmured, "This is Yaghenen. The Spirit of Yaghenen is our life spirit."

He smiled softly as he thought of the Good Land, his homeland of the Kenai Peninsula, as his cousins nodded in agreement. He was filled with the joy of being Denaina. His people were Alaskan Native Athabaskans. The Denaina, called Tanahna by the Russians, were the inhabitants of south central Alaska whose traditional territory reached from inland Sutton to Chickaloon, Talkeetna and Lime Village. The Denaina villages stretched south to Seldovia and Pedro Bay on the coast of the Pacific Ocean.

The Kenai Peninsula projected out from mainland Alaska, surrounded by the Pacific Ocean waters of the Gulf of Alaska to the east and to the western arms of where Tikatnu, or Cook Inlet extended inland. The Denaina lived along both sides of Tikahtnu. Tikahtnu, or Big Water River, stretched from the Gulf of Alaska to the upper reaches of the fifteen mile long Nuti, the Knik Arm. From the north, the great Susitna and the Knik Rivers dumped silty brown currents into the Tikatnu so that the upper reaches were opaque. The Tutl'uh, or Turnagain Arm, was narrower than the Knik Arm and coursed forty five miles from the west side of Tikatnu. Steep mountains stabbed into the sky at six thousand feet of sheer vertical slopes, resembling giants with many glaciers like wraps slung over their shoulders. Several creeks and rivers drained into the Arm, dumping glacial silt when the tide was out, so that the expansive mudflats of Tutl'uh became deadly sinkholes entrapping any creature that wandered out onto the muddy beaches. The world's second highest tide of forty feet poured into the Tutl'uh, a bore tide that roared at five to seven miles per hour with waves of up to ten feet.

Acts Quickly recalled that above the headwaters of the Turnagain Arm was the pass leading to the south towards the main Kenai Peninsula. Mountain goats, Dall sheep, caribou, moose and brown bear inhabited the Peninsula's forests of spruce, alder, cottonwood and birch. The steep pass climbed nine hundred feet among the mountains and eventually descended to Sqilan Bena, the ridge lake place or the Kenai Lake. The lake formed a twenty-two mile

L before draining into the Kahtnu. The Kahtnu, the mighty blue Kenai River, shone aquamarine or turquoise as glacial silt hurled down the turbid currents, sifting out light rays to leave only the blue spectrum. The Kahtnu flowed eighty-two miles westward from the Kenai Lake through another expansive lake, racing down canyons before finally gushing into the ocean waters of Cook Inlet. The world's largest chinook, sockeye, pink and silver salmon spawned in the river in schools of hundreds of thousands, yearly from May until October. Brown bear feasted on the rich oily salmon, so that they grew to the size of giants. The Denaina speared the salmon and dried them for the winter, storing the fish in airtight birch bark baskets. Trout, dolly varden, and whitefish also inhabited the river system, providing a variety of tasty fish. At the mouth of the river, the inlet waters provided an abundance of beluga and seals while the beaches were filled with clams.

Acts Quickly closed his eyes. He called to his mind the time when over a year ago, he had stood in the clearing waiting for his father, his cousins Spear and Last Waters, and the village elder to arrive up river from their village on the flats. The chief's son had finished his vision quest and was ready to return home, a changed young man. He smiled at his cousins as he returned to the moment.

Last Waters stirred, breaking the reverie. "We have to go farther for caribou now. The caribou are hiding back up in the mountains. I haven't seen tracks or signs of wolves or any other fur bearers. Since the invaders, the Russians, have come here, the animals are being killed out of balance." He shook his head.

Last Waters was tall and slim like the chief's son. He resembled his mother, who was known for her incredible beauty and delicate facial features, but his appearance was accentuated by a sinewy, masculine strength. The young women of the village sought to be his friend and enjoyed his company. He was at ease with the flirtations despite the teasing his cousins poured on him over the feminine attention. "The Russians are greedy. They want more furs, more meat, more fish. They take it all away on their ships and only offer vodka for payment. They don't want to share their rifles or ammunition. The land and the ancestors are becoming offended."

Acts Quickly agreed solemnly. He knew that the Denaina had enjoyed life at Yaghenen for thousands of years, thriving on the abundance of furs for clothes and shelter, the fish and animals for food, and the rich flora such as berries or other plants for food or medicine or utensils and tools. The Kahtnuht Dena'ina, or People along the Kenai River, loved the land with great respect of the flora and fauna of their country.

Acts Quickly's father was chief of Shk'ituk't, the village with over a thousand inhabitants located on the lower flats, which in Denaina meant Place Where We Slide Down, on the banks of the Kenai delta near the beaches of Cook Inlet. The people reverenced the spirit of the land as well as the spirits of the animals and plants and all livings things, even of the mountains and rivers. The respect for the land and the spirits was practiced strictly by leaving no mark or evidence of human impact after having lived in a place. Campsites and villages were left with little or no trace of human development. Animals, fish or plants that were harvested were consumed entirely with no waste. The Denaina took gratefully from the land only what he or she needed, and no more. The balance of the land and the Kahtnuht Denaina was abundant and peaceful and plentiful.

Then the Russians had invaded in 1741. They began their invasion of Alaska in the Aleutian Islands, pillaging the resources of otter and seal furs and other animals, as well as enslaving the Alutiiq and Unangan natives there. Then they had moved to the mainland. When they arrived, they demanded furs from the Denaina, as the Native men were expert trappers and hunters.

The Russians had rifles and threatened the people. They built a rudimentary fort, took without asking and showed no respect. The Russians whisked as many furs away as they could load on their ships and came back for more. The Russians paid with vodka, some metal utensils and a few old rifles in the beginning. But quickly, the invaders delayed paying the Denaina and began to enslave them, demanding more and more. The fort became a dump heap and the stench of carcasses hung in the air.

Denaina women feared the brutish ways of the invaders. The men became troubled by the increasing greed of the foreigners and the disrespect they showed to the women and the land. The spirits of the land were becoming disturbed.

Acts Quickly, Spear and Last Waters had left the village the day before and camped overnight so that they could rise before dawn and begin hunting caribou. They were sturdy and well dressed in furs and tanned hides from head to foot. Acts Quickly was the tallest, lithe and remarkably handsome. His easy grin flashed often as he moved like a breeze over the waters fishing or over the land hunting. No one, not even the invading Russians, could resist his sharp wit and humor. As befitting a son of the chief, he excelled in all manner of hunting and fishing, as well as being a natural leader. He was loved by all and men naturally followed him.

"We'll go back down the river and beach before the canyons, then set out on foot to the hills and look for caribou there today," Acts Quickly told his companions.

Spear nodded and bent over to retie the lace on his skin boots. He was much shorter than the chief's son, with broad shoulders and thick arms and legs. His skin was the darkest of the three, his face was already growing a thick mustache and beard, and his white teeth often flashed in a ready grin. Spear was surprisingly fast despite his short legs. He enjoyed showing off his strength and athleticism. He jumped into hard work, such as paddling, lifting heavy moose or caribou quarters, or hauling wood. It was said that Spear would never be found resting at his home in the village between hunts. Spear was always skinning, carving or making something useful such as skin boats for hunting.

The young men's skin boat was pulled up on a small sandbar some hundred yards away from the meadow down the bank and beached on the Kenai River. The blue waters swirled and sang. The Denaina proudly lived along the river.

Acts Quickly, Spear and Last Waters drifted down the river as the dawn broke. They hunted that day, but found only a group of caribou cows and calves. The next day was warm and bright as they continued downriver before landing to trek inland. They found a group of bulls and killed only what they could transport, before bringing the meat back to the village. That night, the villagers gathered to feast and dance. A massive heap of driftwood had been gathered and lit for a bonfire. Joyfully, the Denaina brought clams, whale meat, seal oil and dried fish to share along with baskets of sweet berries.

Acts Quickly rose from his seat by his father and found his mother among the women serving the meal. She affectionately pinched his dimpled cheeks and he flashed a smile at her. He saw the pride in her dark eyes. He felt a wave of relief to see his mother smile again. Ever since the Russians had come and built their fort beyond the village, his mother was upset. Too long had she mourned the loss of his older sister. Too long had she cried in fear of losing him when he left on a hunting trip. But time was healing her loss.

"I'll bring the Spirit across the river some food," Acts Quickly said, as he grabbed a bite of steaming caribou meat from the platter his mother held.

She smiled and nodded towards the edge of the fire before hurrying to bring the meat to her husband. A birch bark basket of meat and fish and berries sat by the fire, ready for the Acts Quickly in anticipation of his generous care. He grabbed up the basket and disappeared down the trail to the river to the waiting skin boat.

The chill dusk of September was falling rapidly as Acts Quickly easily paddled across the river and up the sloughs. It was hard to see across the inlet, as the sun was setting behind the snowcapped peaks of the Alaska Peninsula range when Acts Quickly landed the boat, hopped out, and nimbly jogged up the narrow trail.

The footpath wound up a sloping bluff among alders and black spruce. At the crest of the bluff, the trail curved south into the forest to a small hidden knoll. Acts Quickly set the basket down at the top of the knoll. Then, he ran further south along the trail and, at length, stood on the bluff of the inlet over the waters. He looked for a tall ship anchored offshore. It was empty, but he knew the ship was on its way and would arrive any day now. The Russians at the fort above the village were looking for the ship as well, and talking about the spirits it would bring them from their motherland.

The young man sped forward along the bluffs so he could keep his eyes on the Russian fort on the north bank of the Kenai River. There were lights and tiny shadows of men moving along the edges of the fort. The Russians were running low on food and supplies, but he knew they only wanted one. Vodka. He scoffed. After completing his offering of food to the Spirit, he turned back towards his boat and the village.

The Denaina feasted well late into the night. Then, the Denaina drums were taken out and the careful ceremony of singing began. The fire crackled and lit up the night as the villagers sang. They danced to timeless melodies from the ancients. As the night wore on, dancing and singing gave way to the sukdu or storytelling. Children gathered dozily around elders who reposed near the glowing embers of the driftwood logs. Acts Quickly was wide awake. The story telling was his favorite part of the gathering. He listened intently as the elders told of legends handed down from ancient times. He pictured in his head each scene laid out in the Denaina tongue.

The oldest of the villagers began his oration after a time. He spoke of the story of K'etniyi. Acts Quickly smiled. He had heard this speech retold since he first learned to listen as a toddler. It meant that "it has something to say." Everything in the world of the Denaina, from the rocks to the animals or plants, had a spirit, and the people were taught to listen to the spirits around them. In listening to the spirits, the people learned and practiced respect. In sharing the stories, respect was passed to each generation.

The oldest of the villagers cleared his throat and took a sip of water before beginning his next story. "This is the story of a mouse."

Murmurs of excitement ran through the villagers. Listeners shifted and pulled fur blankets around them and their little ones who were falling asleep one by one. Spear got up and put several logs on the fire. There was a tap on Act's Quickly's shoulder. He glanced up. It was his mother, smiling as she wrapped a warm caribou rug around her son's shoulders. She smoothed his hair before returning to her seat beside his father. His father gently smiled at his son before turning his attention to the elder.

"A long time ago, a young man was tired. All around him, the villagers were busy. They had gathered sturdy poles from young saplings and fashioned them into a fish weir along the river where the currents allowed a man to safely wade and the fish swam through. The people gathered spruce roots and wove nets out of them before attaching them to a long wooden pole. These were the nets they used to dip the salmon out of the weir. Some men preferred to spear the salmon with long, sharply pointed spears. As the salmon began to come in huge schools, the villagers gathered to harvest them for the coming winter. Fish were cut and dried on racks constructed out of poles. Fires were tended under the racks to keep flies away and smoke

portions of the fish. There was great hustle and bustle all along the river and around the village.

The tired young man wandered near the river. Some men muttered that he was lazy. An old woman who sat on the riverbank cutting salmon hollered at him to stop being lazy and help gather food for the winter. She said, 'You'll starve in the long cold months of snow. There won't be any food for you if you don't help.' The villagers all laughed. They quickly turned back to their work and forgot about him.

The young man sank wearily onto a log of driftwood near the fish weir. He watched the men spearing and dipnetting huge salmon out of the waters. Suddenly, he heard a small squeak. He looked around to see where the sound came from. A tiny mouse with a large orange salmon egg in its mouth was struggling to jump over a tree root that blocked its path to the grass further along the bank. The young man smiled. He forgot about his weariness and kindness flooded his heart. 'Here you go.' he whispered, as he picked up the mouse tenderly and set it down near the grasses a foot away. The mouse dashed into the foliage. In his lazy mind, the young man soon forgot about the mouse.

Winter came early that year. The snow fell and icy winds blew. The old woman who had yelled at the young man fell sick. The sickness spread through the village like a wildfire.

One night, the young man listened. The only sound in the village was his stomach growling over the moaning and coughing coming from each dwelling of the villagers. After a sleepless night, the young man got up early. He put on his furs and grabbed a bow with arrows. He set out to find food.

After a long day's journey, the young man was faint with hunger as the sun set. He found a thicket of trees to spend the frigid night in and began trudging towards it. As he entered the thicket, to his surprise, there was a miniature house. A tiny woman appeared at the door. She waved him inside quickly, saying, 'You must be hungry and cold.'

It was warm in the diminutive dwelling, as a fire lit up the room. The smell of delicious soup cooking hit him hard. His stomach growled like a roar. The woman giggled and bade him to sit. She explained that her husband was away but would be back soon. She ladled a large wooden bowl of tasty soup and handed it to the young man. She watched him eat with beady eyes that shone in the firelight.

The young man ate the soup heartily. As he finished, there was a loud noise outside. 'My husband is back,' the woman exclaimed. Slowly, the fur rug over the doorway pulled aside. A gigantic head appeared, followed by shoulders as an extremely large man crawled through the door.

The young man was startled until he saw the kindness in the eyes of the man. He swallowed and settled back. The woman spoke to the large man in a different language and they both looked at the young man. The husband welcomed the young man and set him at ease. The evening passed peacefully, and the young man slept deeply on comfortable furs near the fire with a full stomach.

The next morning, the young man started to explain to the couple of the large man and the tiny wife of how he came to their house while on his way hunting food for his village. He shared how the villagers were sick and starving. He ended his account and started to gather his things to set out in the cold again when the husband stopped him. 'Wait a moment,' said the husband as he lumbered from the room. He returned with a small skin. On the skin, he laid tiny pieces of meat, dried fish, a berry and a fish egg. On top of the miniature food pieces, he laid a white feather. Then, he wrapped up the skin and food into a small bundle. He motioned to the young man to take the bundle. 'When you get near the village, call out to announce your arrival. Spread the skin out with the food pieces on top on the snow. Wave the feather over it. The food will become enough to feed your entire village the rest of the winter. Make a soup with the fish egg. It will heal your people who are sick.'

The young man was speechless. He looked from husband to wife in confusion. The husband laughed. 'I am Gujun. It was me you lifted over the roots that day last summer when I was a mouse carrying a salmon egg home to prepare for the winter. All your fellow villagers were too busy to stop a moment to be kind to me. You were being lazy which is not good, but you were kind and helped me. I am the Spirit that is related to all animals. For your kindness and helping me, I will help you help your people.'

The young man returned home. He laid the skin out and waved the feather over it. Instantly, there was a large skin lying on the snow covered with bountiful food. He called to the villagers. Those people who were well enough came to him. They carried the food home. They made soup according to the young man's instructions and fed it to the sick. The entire village ate and became strong again. The young men recovered their strength and were able to hunt for food to feed the village all the rest of the year. The people learned to treat all things with kindness and respect, even the tiny mouse." The elder ended his story as the listeners chuckled in appreciation.

Acts Quickly and his cousins helped the elder up and back to his house. That night, Acts Quickly lay awake late. He thought about the ancients. He thought about the Russians. Did they have stories told by elders? They must never listen. They had no respect for the land and the spirits.

TWO

MAKE YOURSELF A SHEEP AND THE WOLF will be ready. Nicholas stood on the upper deck, surveying the morning crew as the sailors began checking the rigging and swabbing the decks. He studied the giant Igor from western Estonia, careful not to be caught staring. The monster was swarthy, scarred and dangerous, constantly looking for trouble. Igor had killed a man at the port of Kamchatka in a drunken brawl. He was a bully with powerful arms to match. In a crew of the roughest, hardiest, most seasoned Russian sailors, ex-soldiers and the swarthy rejects of Russian aristocracy and wealthy, Igor was the worst.

Nicholas hadn't let his guard down since boarding the ship of the Russian company Lebedev, which ran furs and other trade goods from Kenai, Alaska, to Russia. Just as the mast of the St. George the Victorious loomed tall and stalwart against the violent storms that raged the Bering Sea, the Aleutian Islands, and Gulf of Alaska, so stood Nicholas, with a razor sharp knife and pistol at the ready on each hip. The young man was only nineteen years of age, his junior officer position bought at a high price by a wealthy and shadowy banker from St. Petersburg, who had insisted on sending the Nicholas to watch over his extensive investment in the Lebedev Company.

Nicholas recalled the day in April when the banker arrived at the orphanage. Nicholas had stood at the window of his room, staring at the cold spring outside. He wondered what would become of himself. He was turning eighteen and would be forced to leave the care of the priests and nuns who raised the orphans. Below, a carriage pulled into the courtyard and a large man dressed in fine furs emerged. He looked up at Nicholas, smiled and waved a hand as a priest rushed from the door to greet the guest. When Nicholas was ushered into the library to meet the visitor, he noticed the large gold ring on his finger as well as a gold chain around his neck. The man said his name was Victor Perov and he owned a bank in St. Petersburg. The man spoke heartily. He had an offer for Nicholas. Nicholas would be provided with training, a fine salary and an officer's rank by the time he turned nineteen. But in return, he needed Nicholas to do something for him. It was a secret mission. Nicholas' thoughts returned to the present as he heard the Captain speaking to him.

"Igor is an animal. I did not want him on my crew. Gregori sent for him," Captain Stephan Zaikov muttered under his breath as he joined the young officer's survey of the crew. Nicholas knew Zaikov was referring to Gregori Konovalov, garrison leader of Redoubt Kenay, or Fort Kenai, their destination.

"Never turn your back on him, Nicholas. Igor is as much of a murderous thug as Gregori is." Nicholas nodded solemnly.

"Join me for breakfast in my cabin," the Captain ordered as he turned. Nicholas saluted the officer, relieving him before making his way to the Captain's cabin.

The Captain sighed heavily as the cook set the small wooden table with hot tea and a spare meal. After the cook left and the meal was consumed, Zaikov settled back in his chair and began to speak. "We will be arriving at the mouth of the inlet in two days. We will continue up the inlet to Redoubt Kenay, the Russian built fort. On the west side of the inlet is Zimov'e Tyonek, a satellite trading post. There, another Russian fort, St. George Redoubt was established by Peter Kolomin, a foreman for the Lebedev Company. Back in 1787, Kolomin arrived on the vessel St. Paul. There were almost forty men with him. He later sailed to the mouth of the Kasilof River, which is twelve miles south along the eastern shore of the inlet from Fort Kenai."

Zaikov stood and pointed to a chart on the wall of the cabin. "We are going to the St. Nicholas Redoubt," the Captain said, tapping his finger on the chart at the delta of a larger river.

Nicholas poured more tea as the Captain settled back in his chair. Zaikov recounted the history carefully. It was the first time the Captain had been able to speak at length to the young man since he joined the crew as an officer. Nicholas listened attentively to the Captain, noting the man's concern. The Russian sea Captain had been sailing to Alaska for decades now. He had extensive knowledge, having previously been a scholar, unbeknownst to his uncouth peers in the Lebedev Company. Zaikov was also a tall man, whose square shoulders and august face inspired natural obeisance from all his crew. He generated courage and quick thinking, which drew respect from the roughest or most debased of crew man. The men of the Lebedev company were ruthless for the most part, being fugitives, army soldiers, and outcast thugs seeking their fortune in Alaska. It was rare to find a man who was aristocratic or educated or principled. Most managers or captains ruled by fear and force, which made Zaikov an exception. The majority of captains were wild men sent by the Czar Peter the Great of Russia to a wild land to ravage resources for trade with China and to provide the Russian empire with badly needed riches.

Zaikov settled back into his chair and recounted to Nicholas the history of the Russian expansion into Alaska, which had started with the explorations of Vitus Bering and Aleksei Chirikov in 1728 and 1741. In the islands of the Bering Sea and the Aleutians, the Russians had begun a fur trade, building forts which they called redoubts. Companies had formed and trade had expanded to the coast of south-central Alaska and up the inlet made famous after the 1778 voyage of the British explorer James Cook. Zaikov noted that even the Spanish sailed the inlet in 1788, but their claims for the Spanish empire were ignored.

The first redoubt in the Cook Inlet region was built at the mouth of the Kasilof River. In 1791, however, another redoubt named St. Nicholas was built at the mouth of the Kenay, or Kenai River. The project was led by Gregori Konovalov and his sidekick, Amos Balushin, after the two managers had failed to get along with the Lebedev company men at Redoubt St. George. But Konovalov's methods of trading had brought the Russians and Native peoples to violence, breaking the trade relations carefully built by the Lebedev manager at the redoubt on the Kasilof River. Native peoples were enslaved and mistreated brutally by the company men. Zaikov shook his head in disapproval.

"That's why I am going to Redoubt Kenay. Complaints from the other redoubts are reaching St. Petersburg. Father Juvenal, a missionary priest from the Valaam Monastery near St. Petersburg, and his monks visited St. Nicholas Redoubt earlier this year. He sent the reports of Konovalov back to St. Petersburg. He wanted them arrested and removed to Russia to stand trial. There is pressure on the Lebedev managers to keep their men in control and to practice better relations with the Native people. If the situation is as bad as the Orthodox priest says, I have orders to take command." Zaikov paused.

He studied the young officer soberly. Nicholas was taller

than the Captain, broad shouldered, muscular, with a dangerous intensity. Smooth skin and a rosy blush on the cheeks belied Nicholas's age, but the Captain knew the officer was well trained and able to overcome anyone who would challenge him, even Igor. The young officer was a contradiction, with aristocratic features yet powerfully built like a fearless fighter, younger than all the men on the ship but poised as if he had a powerful commission and great authority, and strangely out of place butyet quiet and unassuming. He preferred to remain in the background.

"When do we arrive?" Nicholas asked.

"In about four days, if the weather holds." Zaikov rose and pointed to the chart again. "We will be entering the inlet tonight. The tides are treacherous. The inlet is filled with clay mud from the volcanic peaks on the western side. The English explorer Captain James Cook lost an anchor offshore in the mud back in '94 when he stopped here."

He tapped a point of land south of Kenay on the chart. "We will have to go slowly. It is rare that a vessel sails from Russia to Redoubt Kenay so late in September. But fortunately, the weather has been permissible."

Zaikov paused a moment. Just as he began to ask a question, there was a rap on the door. Nicholas felt a wave of relief. He knew that the Captain was curious about him, and would gently prod to understand why someone so young was a high-ranking officer, and what reason would impel an aristocrat to go to such a horrible place as the remote, violent, cold stench of St. George Redoubt. It was the Orthodox Hieromonk at the door. The head of the Orthodox missionaries from the Valaam monastery, Father Ioasaf, had also come to investigate the situation at St. George and the possibility of establishing a mission there. Father Ioasaf rarely left his cabin, having struggled to overcome severe seasickness. He was pale and weak.

Nicholas recalled the soft tap on his door that had woken him in the late watch of the night after the ship had left Kamchatka. He had opened it to find the Father, holding a finger to his lips. The monk's black kobuk, or veiled hat, and his zostikon, or cassock, and vest, or kontorasson, were one with the shadows. His face, which was narrow and long, eerily pale and thin, with a severe aesthetic air, peered at him. He was tall and lean, yet there was a strength about him that resembled the commanding presence of Zaikov. He was a man of a different kind of authority that demanded respect from the rough men. His gold cross shone on his breast. He motioned for Nicholas to follow him to his cabin. Safely inside the room, the monk spoke softly and urgently to the young officer. Two years earlier in 1794, the esteemed Father Juvenal , a priest from the same Valaam Monastery as Father Ioasaf, had been sent to find a community to begin an Orthodox mission, before a team of monks would follow to establish an enduring presence in the Prince William Sound and Kenai Peninsula regions. Father Juvenal had sent promising reports of baptizing the Native peoples of the area. However, he also reported troubling cruel treatment and unchristian behavior of the Russian fur traders. Enslavement, murder, and stealing Native women for sex slavery, as well as extortion for furs and general cruelty were recorded. In his final report, Father Juvenal spoke of something most urgent, requesting the presence of the leader. Then, all communications had ceased from the Orthodox clergy at St. Nicholas Redoubt. No mention of the monk was in the reports from the Lebedev company either. So, Father Ioasaf was on his way to find out what Father Juvenal could only tell him in person.

"You look like a man of principle and faith." Father Ioasaf eyed the young Nicholas carefully. "I have watched you grow at the orphanage. The priests were pleased with the man you grew up to be.

Perhaps you will help me when we land. Watch my back so to speak." The monk's words hung pointedly in the close air of the cabin.

Nicholas had grown up in the orphanage of the missionaries at Valaam. He did not know Father Ioasaf, but he had met Father Juvenal at the mission. As a young boy, Nicholas had been held captive by the priest's sermons describing an intense love of preaching to the foreign missions. He knew the Heiromonk who was now peering at him intently was curious about him and wanted to know how a poor ophan from the mission had become an officer on the vessel, but he didn't respond to the bait. He was not in the mood to explain his reason for sailing to Alaska.

He spoke lightly, "If I can be of any assistance, good Father, I will be most happy to." With that, the priest turned and abruptly left the tiny quarters.

Now, in Captain Zaikov's presence, the priest ignored the young officer. There was a stiff formality between the company man and the clergy man. "Captain, I see we are entering the inlet. Let us stop at the Zimove at Tyonek and see how things are. Perhaps Father Juvenal is there. It is on our way."

Zaikov shook his head. "I am sorry. The weather is about to change. We must proceed to Kenai directly. It is for the same reason we did not stop in Tri Sviatitelia, the Three Saints."

He was referring to the recent route in which the ship had sailed directly through the Strait named for Grigori Shelikhov to the mouth of Cook Inlet, bypassing the post of Shelikhov Trading Company and its nearby Orthodox mission of Three Saints on Glotov, or Kodiak Island. Since it was late in the year for sailing, Zaikov was intent on reaching their destination as quickly as possible.

Nicholas nodded to each man and exited the cabin, leaving them to argue about the itinerary. He paused a moment so his eyes could adjust to the dark passageway. Suddenly, all the light was blocked. There stood Igor. It was same man who Captain Zaikov, while on deck, had just warned Nicholas to avoid. Igor had entered the narrow passageway and stopped short. He stared at the young officer, his massive face paling, his ugly eyes staring as if he had seen a ghost.

"Someone is with the Captain now," Nicholas said curtly and moved past the frozen giant who stood dumbly by. He made his way to his quarters to rest. He sank immediately into a deep dreamless slumber.

The first rays of the crisp September dawn found Nicholas on deck. He was studying the geography of the inlet. The ocean waters had come to be named as Cook Inlet two years earlier in 1794, for the previous 1778 exploratory voyage of the famed Englishman Captain Cook as who had searched for the Northwest Passage in service of the British Empire. The Tertiary and Cretaceous Eras, as well as ancient Paleozoic complexes, made up the inlet's composite terrain. A series of recently active volcanoes rose as mighty snowcapped mountains along the great western peninsula: Mount Augustine, Mount Illiamna, then the tallest Mount Redoubt, and finally, Mount Spur, nearest the head of the inlet. Great bluffs rose from the water level along most of the shore. Lowlands of glacial and volcanic deposits composed the flats on either side of the inlet. The fall had begun to arrive on the land. Forests of deciduous birches, willows and alders stood with an erect presence as if soldiers in gold uniforms among officers of dark uniforms, the evergreens of spruce and hemlock. Nicholas appreciated the beauty, the blue sky above and the crisp wind gently filling the sails. However, the beauty was deceptive. Great rocks and silty bars demanded careful navigation on the forceful bore tide, whose currents roared into and out of the inlet as powerful as a swift river. Captain Cook had mistaken the body of water for a giant river due to these dramatic tidal currents on his previous exploratory venture.

Captain Zaikov joined Nicholas with his eyeglass tucked under his arm. He pointed out where the posts of Illiamna and Tyonek were located on the far side of the inlet. They passed St. George Redoubt and the mouth of the Kasilof River. The men busied themselves readying for the arrival to St. Nicholas Redoubt on the Kenai. Nicholas peered at the shore. The river mouth was much larger than he expected. As the ship sailed on, the Denaina village came into view. On the north shore, he could see dozens of canoes banked on the first bend of the river and a cluster of log cabins above the grassy tidal zone, while the fort on the bluff loomed ominously above the beach directly at the point where the river met the inlet waters. Zaikov explained that the Native village was a small distance away from the fort, in a wooded flat below a gentle slope from the river. These were the Dena'ina. They called themselves the Kahtnuht'ana. The Russians referred to them as Kenaitze, the People of the Flats. Suddenly, despite the distance and roar of the tide, the shoreline filled with activity and noise. Dogs barked, children laughed, and men yelled as people poured out of the cabins of the Denaina village and the gate of the fort.

St. George the Victorious set anchor well offshore, while the sails were pulled up and boats were lowered. Zaikov, the officers, and the priest arrived on shore in the first boat. They paddled up the river into the mouth of a small stream that ran along under the bluff. The trail up the bluff was dusty and men from the fort came eagerly running down it to greet the landing party.

God keeps those safe who keep themselves safe. The men from the fort were unkempt and armed. Nicholas glanced at Zaikov, who met his gaze and nodded almost imperceptibly. Be careful to watch your back and everyone around, the Captain seemed to be saying. Even the dogs from the fort were large, mangy and matted, growling and snarling at the crew of the vessel as they disembarked. The men from the fort greeted the landing party with cursing and rough language, crudely joking about how long it took the ship to finally arrive and where the fresh stores of vodka were. Zaikov barked a command in Russian and the men started. It was then that they noticed the priest who quietly stood behind the Captain. The second skiff beached just then, filled with Zaikov's crew. Zaikov directed the first mate to oversee the unloading and began up the trail, motioning Nicholas and the monk to come with him.

"Where's Konovalov?" Zaikov demanded of a man rushing past them on the trail down to the shore. The man pointed up the bluff and said they could find him in the officers' quarters in the main house in the fort.

"Why isn't he here to greet us?" Zaikov muttered as he resumed his ascent.

The monk covered his nose with his sleeve. Trash, rotted carcasses of salmon and animals, and filth lined either side of the trail. It was difficult to climb and breathe in the stench. Stands of cottonwood trees, bordered by fire weed that had gone to seed, covered the steep slope. Behind them, the beach grass, now dried and golden, rustled in the evening breeze which swept from the cold inlet waters to the bluff top where the sunlight still slanted in warm rays.

The wooden gate of the fort stood at the peak of the bluff. It was in disrepair. Rough slats of wood were broken and it appeared the gate could not be secured completely shut. The fort interior was dirty and chaotic, like the trail leading up the bluff.

Zaikov swiftly led the way to the officers' barracks, a two-story building fashioned from the Russian custom of squaring the spruce timbers. It was chinked with clay and there were one or two oilskin covered windows that were sullen and dark. The men entered, pausing a moment as their eyes adjusted to the gloom. The close air was heavy with sweat, wood and pipe smoke, vodka, and yet more rotting meat or fish. Crudely hewed wooden tables and benches stood at one end of the room, and the cooking area took up the rest. Rough stairs led to the second story. A makeshift desk stood under the window that looked to the southwest over the beach.

As their eyes adjusted, they became aware of the man in the shadows beyond the large iron wood stove that took up most of the cooking area. The man's look reminded Nicholas of a wolverine he had once seen in a cage at the Valaam market. Dangerous. Amused. The man had taken advantage of their temporary blindness and studied them for weakness, giving him a slightly sardonic and arrogant light in his cold deadly eyes. He was squat, with a block shaped head covered in short blond hair, a cruel looking square face, and chilling pale blue eyes. He looked powerfully built despite his short stature.

Zaikov was irritated at being scrutinized. "Amos Balushin." the Captain did not disguise his disgust. "You old snake. Hiding there in the dark like a devil."

Balushin stepped forward, sheathed a long knife at his hip and wiped his hands on his filthy pants. He opened his mouth to speak, but Zaikov cut him short, "Where's your boss? Where's Konovalov?" Balushin smirked and pointed up the stairs.

"What have you done to him, you wolf?" Zaikov drew himself up dangerously tall. His officers moved to his side. Balushin waved his hand dismissively. Without speaking, he pointed again to the stairs. He gave a hideous snicker.

Zaikov led the way up the stairs. The second floor was as rough as the first. Each corner held a bed. Rough boards made some attempt at partitioning the area. The only windows looked over the fort yard and the trail head from the beach. The air would have been unbearable if the gaps between the boards didn't allow a chill current in. The bed covers were comprised of filthy worn furs.

A moan emitted from the far corner. The men rushed to the bedside. There lay a giant form under a pile of furs. The air reeked of vodka. An empty bottle lay sideways on the floor beside the bed. Snoring filled the room.

"He finished the last of the vodka this morning. He figured you were coming today and he planned that you would bring more." Balushin's voice startled them from behind as he stood with a smirk. "He is not available today to greet you."

Zaikov turned. "Start cleaning this filthy place up and finish by tonight," he demanded.

As he passed Balushin, his hand shot up as if he meant to soundly backhand the shorter man. Balushin flinched and ducked. Zaikov swept downstairs. Balushin blushed deeply and stood with his head bowed in wretched shame as the men filed past and followed the Captain down the stairs.

By the time the darkness of the September night fully engulfed the fort, the officers' quarters were cleaned and accommodations were made for all the men of rank. Stores were replenished as loads were oared from the ship and carried up the bluff. Curious Denaina came up from the village to watch the proceedings. Several young Denaina stopped Balushin along the trail from the beach as he helped unload supplies. They wanted to give word that the chief of the village had extended an invitation to the "new Russian Captain." Balushin relayed the message to the Captain, and Zaikov sent a response back to the Denaina that he would meet with the chief in the coming days.

Fresh coho salmon which still swam up from the ocean late into September had been hastily netted from the river, and a feast of fish with bacon and vegetables was laid for the hungry men. Captain Zaikov ate heartily and sat back, watching his crew mingle with the men of the fort through narrow eyes. Nicholas was seated next to the monk, who had said little after blessing the meal. The young officer was aware of the change in Zaikov since they landed. He realized the Captain was a capable and formidable man, well suited to command the rough men of the fort.

After eating his fill, Nicholas wandered outside the officers' quarters to the courtyard in the middle of the fort. The night air was chilly and cutting as a stiff breeze blew up the bluff from the inlet water and over the wooden walls. Men were lounging about in the shadows and porches of the barracks. He had learned from Konovalov that each night, two watchmen kept a fire in the court-yard, ready to sound the alarm for any dangers.

The Russians were nervous about the Natives, having heard many tales of attacks on redoubts by the indigenous men of the Aleutian and Kodiak Islands in previous decades. Nicholas spotted Igor talking to Balushin. The men were engaged in animated conversation for several minutes before noticing the young man watching. He could barely make out their words.

"No. We can't get the women from the village in here tonight for the men. Zaikov will have us all arrested for abusing the natives. You know what happened to the women. Konovalov is terrified. He is losing his mind over this. Zaikov will send him home, you see," Balushin was saying.

Igor's thick bass voice retorted, "No. I am here now. No one sends Gregori anywhere when I am here."

They suddenly stopped, aware of Nicholas watching and stared at him directly. Balushin said something out of the corner of his mouth. Igor began to stand up, his giant bulk menacing in the half-lit yard.

"I am to sleep in the officers' quarters tonight. What do you think of that? Am I a child who can't take care of himself?" It was Father Ioasaf who spoke softly, stepping out of the doorway of the officers' quarters from behind. He joined Nicholas.

"It is best to be careful. It is wise to listen to Captain Zaikov," Nicholas replied as he kept an eye on Igor, his hand instinctively dropping to his knife sheath. But his tenseness was soon calmed, as at the sound of the priest's voice, Igor and Balushin retreated further into the shadows until they disappeared. The monk sighed deeply. "No sign of Father Juvenal. No church built yet, just a dingy one room shack with no accommodations they showed me. That's where they put Father Juvenal. That's how they welcomed the Church into the fort. Holy Liturgy in a shack."

"This fort is a shack. How can it even be called a fort, it is a disgrace. Where is your Father Juvenal? Why isn't he here to greet and welcome you?" Nicholas queried.

The monk shook his head. "I am very worried. I don't know what is going on. Balushin made a comment that Father Juvenal preferred the Denaina. He hinted about a woman. He said the cleric kept busy with efforts to baptize the 'heathens'. Apparently, Father Juvenal stayed in the village and kept traveling among the native villages, even across the inlet. I think there was tension between Konovalov and Father over something."

In a flash, the monk's hand shot out to Nicholas, clutching at his chest. His fingers sought and gripped the cross around Nicholas' neck that was hidden by his clothes. Nicholas laid his hand over the monk's hand and they stood face to face a moment.

"I will help you as much as I can without compromising my mission, Father," Nicholas hissed under his breath.

The priest answered, "What is your mission? I knew who you were the minute I laid eyes on you. Zaikov wonders who you really are. Now," he twisted the cross, "I know for sure. Why are you here?"

Nicholas drew a breath. "I will help you, Father, as much as I am able without arousing suspicions, but I cannot tell you why I am here. If you love your country and your Patriarch, you will not tell anyone what you think you know."

He roughly shoved the monk's hand off his chest and looked around to see if anyone was watching. "After all, we are all on the same side. Your missionaries trained me well. You don't doubt my devotion?"

The monk shook his head. He continued to speak softly, now pleading, "Then, you will come with me tomorrow into the village. We must ask the natives where Father Juvenal is. If he is across the inlet, perhaps you can take me to him?"

Nicholas shook his head. "Remember what I said. Only if I am able."

The monk softened. A group of men could be heard approaching from the fort gate, their drunken voices raised in fear.

To avoid any suspicions, Father Ioasaf made it look like he was praying over Nicholas. "Bless you, my son," the monk continued loudly as he placed his hand on the young man's head. "Sleep well."

Calls erupted from the men passing by. "Bless me too, Father." a man called out. "There is a ghost out there."

The men were stammering at the same time, intoxicated with the newly arrived vodka and incoherent. Nicholas managed to discern something about a white figure appearing on the far side of the river, with a wailing that froze a man's blood, its screams carried across on the winds.

One of the younger members of the frightened crowd broke free and stumbled as he ran to where Nicholas and the monk stood, falling on his knees before Father Ioasaf. "Father, come see."

He caught the monk's hand and tugged, begging in terror, "Come see the ghost and send it away."

"Calm down, son." the priest said softly, reassuring the young man as he patted his hand.

The young man rose and pulled the monk after him towards the gate and the top of the bluff. Nicholas followed, filled with curiosity. The rest of the men jostled and stumbled behind them.

"There," a man cried as he pointed towards the far side of the river.

Nicholas caught his breath. A light was moving along the far shore. He squinted. Was that a figure in white? Instantly, the light disappeared, and a heavy darkness enveloped the entire river and beach. Even the lights of the great vessel moored offshore were impossible to discern as a chill fog swiftly blew in. Father Ioasaf murmured a prayer under his breath.

"You saw it. You saw it," the men stammered loudly around the monk and Nicholas. They all peered into the darkness a long silent moment before hustling back into the fort. The men went quietly to bed, while Nicholas and the monk went back to the officers' quarters.

"Strange." Nicholas looked inquiringly at the priest.

"Very. We must tell Captain Zaikov in the morning," Father Ioasaf replied. He quietly opened the door and gently ascended the stairs to his bed.

THREE

THE MORNING SKY IN ALASKA LIGHTENS after the deepest watches of the arctic night fade. The nocturnal breezes suddenly vanish. Then, mysteriously, the sky dims and the air becomes bitter and despairingly cold. Creatures shiver while every fiber of their being cries out for the sun to hasten and warm the earth. The stillness of this darkest hour before dawn is interminable. Then, like the first morning of creation, a brave angel now winged in feathers mounts that wood of salvation, the highest limb of tree beneath heaven, and sings, recalling that resurrection of creation in the rising of the Son. The bird's first note pierces the darkness and despair of the frozen hearts below. Then, as if summoned by the glorious hymn, the sun begins his ascent, promising warmth and life and the joyous beginning of a new day.

It was at this caliginous predawn, that Nicholas awoke. He froze, trying to get his bearings. The young man had made his bed under the stairway, facing the door and in the deep shadows of the corner. His knife and pistol were beside him, in ready reach.

Sleep had been dilatory, crowded out by his uneasiness. He had lain listening to the snores and grunts of the officers upstairs, pondering the men's near hysteric claims that there was a ghost near the river. Was it the Denaina? Was it drunken fear? Even the priest had made his bed upstairs with the other men. Was he afraid of spirits here? The priest's words came back to the young man. He could not help remembering. He had had a remarkable and unusually clear memory of even the earliest years of his life. Despite being a nameless orphan, he knew exactly who he was. His father had been the highest ranking general in the Preobrazhensky Regiment, the security forces of the Czar. His mother was a lesser royal of the Romanov court. He sighed as he thought of his mother. He could see her beautiful face, hear her gentle voice and feel her warm embrace.

He replayed his mother's last words as she handed him to the Orthodox nuns at Valaam. "Your father is a good man, Nicholas. Remember that. Never forget. He did what was right. He tried to protect the rightful Czar."

She kissed his forehead. "Our family has always served the Czar. You will protect the true Czar when you are a man." Then, she left.

The nuns were kind to him. He waited patiently for his parents to come back and take him home to St. Petersburg. Days passed into months, months passed into years. One day, he insisted on knowing where his parents were. The nuns reluctantly told him. His father had refused to help Catherine become Czarina. So she had him killed. Shortly after his mother hid him at the orphanage, she too was murdered. The reign of Catherine had begun.

The Czarina never found the son of the Regiment commander who resisted her coup of the Russian throne. Meanwhile, Nicholas had excelled in his studies. The wise nuns helped him channel his anger over losing his parents into military training. The hidden network of Russians who opposed Catherine watched the boy grow. When he was turning old enough to be forced to leave the orphanage, the wealthy banker in St. Petersburg had come for him. He was needed for a great task. Nicholas had promised to keep his assignment secret even at penalty of death.

Nicholas stared into the darkness under the stairs as he drew his mind back from memory. He wondered about the ghost and how it might affect his task. At last, Nicholas had fallen into a fitful sleep with deep dreams of faraway places and homes that were warm and bright.

Returning his thought to the present, Nicholas' brain rapidly assessed the situation. A bird song pierced the air outside the oilskin window. Was that what woke him? No. There was a looming shadow in the corner of the kitchen. The man was not aware of the Nicholas' stare on his back or his makeshift bed under the stairs. He leaned over a waste bucket and spit. The man was sick. He straightened and paused, listening to hear if any of the men upstairs had wakened at the sound of his retching. Satisfied, he strode swiftly to the door and softly left. Nicholas noiselessly donned his clothes and pulled up his boots, belting his holster and knife sheath as he himself slipped quietly out the door.

Dying embers were all that were left of the fire and there was no sign of the night watchmen. But there. In the gloom, the man staggered towards the exit and let himself out of the fort, unheeded by the dogs sleeping near the men's barracks. He seemed to be heading to the trail down the bluff to the beach. Nicholas tiptoed to the entrance of the fort. Following, he kept a safe distance behind the man. He could see the man was tall and broad shouldered. His shuffling gait betrayed his heaviness. Nicholas had to run swiftly to the top of the bluff to keep up at a stealthy distance.

The wind at the top of the bluff was cutting. The icy breezes had cleared the fog of the previous night. The mountains loomed over the far side of the inlet, their glaciers barely visible in the dark. The distant ship was devoid of lights and barely distinguishable as it lay anchored offshore. The land and ocean were silent, except for the regular piercing of the bird song from a weather-beaten spruce tree along the top of the bluff. It sounded as if the bird was desperately trying to fight off the dark and cold by itself. Nicholas paused at the top of the trail. He crouched to avoid being silhouetted against the fading stars and lightening gray of dawn, but his caution was unfounded. The man suddenly lurched forward and, grunting loudly, rolled down the bluff and off the trail through the fire weed, until coming to a stop near the creek bank. The wind carried his moaning and crying up the bluff to Nicholas. The young man crept to a stand of several young cottonwood that stood over the beach, several yards off the trail in the middle of the bluff. Nicholas sat down so that he could view the area below while remaining hidden among the dried grasses and fire weed under the leafless cottonwood.

Nicholas pulled his overcoat tighter around him. There was a threat of bitter chill in the breeze stirring from the inlet waters to the west. His view from the bluff was expansive, from the river delta flats and mouth and across the waters to the mountains that rimmed the western shore. The tide was falling. Far beyond the shallows lay the vessel St. George anchored, now with a flickering light aboard but too far to hear any voices of the wakening sailors. A series of staggering glaciated mountain peaks walled the far side of the inlet, each looming over ten thousand feet. He could see from their summits that they were the volcanoes he had studied on the map. The peak directly across the inlet from the fort was like a pyramid in shape, a wisp of steam from one of the volcanic vents billowing into the clear morning air. It was overwhelmingly and starkly beautiful.

Groans and rustling from the shrubs below drew his attention back to the figure Nicholas now recognized. It was Konvalov, the same man he had seen passed out in the bed the day before. The inebriated Russian staggered to his feet and stumbled across the beach grass to the sand. He began to wail and shriek loudly, facing the far shore and jabbing his finger in the air. Nicholas strained to make out the tortured words.

"Show yourself." Great sobs. "Forgive me." Screams. "Stop haunting us." The man collapsed to his knees in the sand, heaving with sobs and curdling wails. The tide proceeded to drop in waves lapping out from the river. The sunlight tipped the volcanic peaks. It was an eerie moment.

Nicholas considered whether he should go to Konovalov and attempt to calm him. When he made to move, a scuffle on the gravel trail stayed him. He ducked and peered through the shrubs. Amos Balushin was descending the trail with his attention fixed on the man weeping on the sandy shore below. Igor lumbered heavily behind at his heels, like a giant, stupid dog.

"Here. Here." Balushin chided Konovalov as he approached him. He motioned to Igor to pick the man up. "Get ahold of yourself."

Igor handily raised Konovalov and put an arm around his shoulders, half dragging him along the trail. Midway up the bluff, Balushin paused and surveyed the inlet. He pointed to the vessel offshore and spoke to the pair. Nicholas struggled to make out the words.

Balushin turned up the trail and spoke loudly, "Captain Zaikov calls a meeting of all the men. Come along. You don't want the Captain to be delayed because of your white ghost. He will be frightened to know the fort is haunted. Or he will think you are mad."

Igor laughed and repeated mockingly, "Captain Zaikov."

Konovalov coughed and gagged as the giant yanked him up the trail.

Nicholas frowned. He watched as the trio crowned the bluff and disappeared. The sun's rays broke over the bluff top. As the air warmed by the sun rushed down the slope the wind changed direction, reversing the chill back across the inlet waters from the mouth of the river. He studied the river, for as like the sunlit air stream, the currents had changed.

To the south, across the river, sunlight touched the distant bluff opposite him. The bluff was much lower than the slope he sat on. It was covered with spruce trees which graduated into birch on the slope, and then into willows, with an occasional spruce stunted by the battering winds and tides among the grasses. The shores were at first appearance sandy, but it was deceptive. A clay silt from ancient volcanic eruptions layered the area with a sticky, slick dark gray muck. A sour smell of decaying salmon that had died after spawning and to floated down the river to wash up on the tide began to waft up from below. White seagulls arrived with the dawn, alighting on the far beaches and crying mournfully. Chickadees fluttered from bush to bush around him, like children giggling. A somber eagle soared along the crest of the bluff up the river. Two ravens began a gliding game of chase, whirling in the sunshine. A murder of crows stirred somewhere around the riverbank, as a black and white magpie swooped down the bluff to investigate something in the grasses.

The airs swirled around Nicholas as he sat in the bushes on the bluff, surveying the river world below him. Warm, teasing air streams played along the bluff with mouthwatering hints of raspberries and rose hips, coming from the bushes whose luscious fruits had long fallen from them or been eaten by birds in the weeks before. Nippy chills stirred from remaining shadows and countered the berries' scent with a musty smell of dying leaves and grasses. A spider climbed a blade of grass beside his knee. Nicholas smiled. This land was not so very different from his motherland of Russia.

Despite the sudden burst of sunlight and activity, Nicholas strained to listen. What was it? His eyes squinted searchingly as he examined the far shore for signs of the ghostly figure from the previous night. He could hear his heart pounding in his chest. Then, he realized what it was that was demanding his attention. It was the silence. The river currents that met with the inlet had quieted as if turned off. The tide had exposed expanses of sandy silty bars as it neared the lowest levels. The waters were muted. Nicholas peered out at the vessel anchored offshore. Mirages played about it in the early sun. Beyond the awakening river delta, far above the inlet, the mountains loomed ever larger. Suddenly, another wisp of steam escaped the vent on Mount Redoubt. Everything transformed from the tranquil wakening moments to an intangible uneasiness. He stirred and froze. There was a soft chuckle from the bushes behind him.

FOUR

NICHOLAS' HEAD JERKED AROUND, HIS SHARP eyes darting left and right as his right hand went to his pistol. He squinted through the grasses and bushes around him as he slowly drew the firearm up, unsure which direction the giggle had come from. For a moment, he wondered if it was a voice or some strange animal that he had heard. He waited, his ears straining. The wind danced mischievously down the slope, rattling twigs and dying leaves, rustling grasses and bending bushes. It swirled as if it too were laughing at him. The image of a ghost watching him and laughing filled his mind and he immediately rejected it.

"Your face." Mirth that had been restrained too long escaped. Below Nicholas and to his right, a golden-brown face smiled at him, breaking free of the bushes. It was a stunningly handsome young man.

"Please don't shoot. I mean no harm."

The man put up his hands in a display of peace and, still laughing, rose. His hair was black and shiny as a raven's wing, falling shoulder length with a neat leather headband. His teeth were even and white, his nose well formed between two deep brown eyes that were warm and friendly. He spoke perfect Russian. Although he couldn't contain his amusement, his laughter was not mocking or unkind. He was dressed in tanned hides that blended perfectly with the foliage. A large knife was sheathed in a handsome leather case on his belt. His broad shoulders were crossed by a bandoleer intricately adorned with beads and fringe, crossed by another strap with a bag that hung smartly at his hip, also beautifully ornate with intriguing designs of bone and glass beads. His long-fingered hands were graceful and yet strong. Nicholas discerned in surprise that Acts Quickly was near his own height. His lithe movement conveyed a manly power despite his teenage youthfulness. As the Russian studied the Acts Quickly, he realized the young man was also inspecting him.

Nicholas chuckled in spite of himself. "You surprised me."

Acts Quickly stepped up to the bank to sit like a conspirator in hiding and settled down with Nicholas in the bushes.

"I am Qadanalchen," he said in a friendly manner. "In your language, my name is Acts Quickly."

He paused before continuing. "My father is the chief of the Kenay. We are Denaina. I am 18 years old."

He glanced at Nicholas and added curiously, "You came on the ship yesterday?"

Nicholas nodded. He shared his name and shook the Acts Quickly's hand. "I came with Captain Zaikov to see how the men are doing at the fort."

Before Nicholas could react, the young Denaina's hand shot out as if to strike his head. Acts Quickly held his hand out to show a spider he had snatched from Nicholas' hair. He laughed again, a low intoxicating laugh.

"See, I am Acts Quickly." He leaned into Nicholas and chided him gently, "You thought I was going to hit you. But, even if I was, I was too quick for you."

Nicholas snorted, half in amusement and half in chagrin.

"Russian traders beat my people," Acts Quickly said simply. "They hit us all the time. They take our women. Treat us like dogs."

Nicholas was shocked and could not speak.

"The new Russian officer sits in the bushes, hiding, watching Konovalov. But Acts Quickly sees everything that goes on. Maybe the new Russian officer and his Captain will stop the bad Russian men from beating my people. Maybe things will change around here now."

Nicholas remained silent, trying to take in the young man's words. He studied Acts Quickly through narrowed eyes, attempting to read the Denaina's thoughts, as he had never before encountered someone so candid. Beyond the bluff, seagulls began shrieking as they gathered on the exposed mudflats left bared by the retreating tide.

Acts Quickly plucked a straw and chewed on it as he stared forward across the river towards the far shore. An enormous smile crossed his face and he turned to Nicholas. "You watch Konovalov go crazy? What do you think? Is he crazy?" He chuckled deeply and continued without waiting for an answer.

"I know why Konovalov goes crazy." With a triumphant look, he announced, "The ghost. The lady all in white who screams over there." He pointed, "She is calling to him."

The Denaina surveyed Nicholas' face a moment for his reaction before leaning into him, his face inches away.

"I know why." Nicholas involuntarily pulled back, his heart beginning to race. He felt irritated with himself for reacting to the Denaina's words, but his tone disturbed him deeply and he didn't understand.

Acts Quickly opened his mouth to continue but stopped short as his head jerked back.

"Nicholas. Nicholas. Hey." It was Amos Balushin bellowing from the trail head on top of the bluff.

Nicholas snorted in disgust.

Acts Quickly grinned and whispered, "He is loud."

Instantly, Acts Quickly's face became serious as he peered through the bushes at Balushin, who took a step down, yelled for Nicholas, and paused a moment before repeating. It sounded like Balushin was cursing lowly.

"He is a bad man, that Russian. You be careful around him. Watch your back." Acts Quickly gave Nicholas a friendly pat on the back.

Nicholas nodded as the Denaina whispered again, "I will find you later and explain to you why Konovalov is going crazy. Why the ghost screams on the shore. Why the men are afraid. But you must go now. Balushin will not stop until he finds you."

Nicholas found himself burning with curiosity to know how Acts Quickly would explain the ghost and Konovalov. He glanced up the trail at Balushin and turned back to whisper a time and place to meet to the Denaina. Acts Quickly was gone.

FIVE

Nicholas DUCKED LOW AND CRAWLED DOWN the slope, careful to remain hidden from Balushin's view. He crept around the bluff face to where the sandy shores of the inlet ended and the incline dropped directly onto the riverbank, before sliding noiselessly down to the jumbled smooth stones along the currents' edge. Balushin yelled louder and descended almost to the cottonwoods along the trail. Nicholas drew himself up, hastily brushed leaves and stems from his hair and clothes and then sauntered unhurriedly around the riverbank into view.

"There you are," Balushin greeted him in an accusing tone.

Nicholas plucked a straw from the edge of the path on his way up the trail to the cottonwoods. He stopped a stride short of the man sent to find him. Even though he was a step below Balushin, who blocked the trail, he towered over the shorter squat man. He stared coldly into Balushin's eyes until Balushin blinked and turned aside.

"The priest is holding liturgy. Captain Zaikov wants all the men to attend. Captain says it is mandatory. And there is confession before the liturgy." Balushin's tone hinted a slight contempt.

Nicholas stepped long past the junior officer and with long strides went up the trail easily. Balushin paused, squinting at the riverbank from where Nicholas had come.

He muttered under his breath, casting a long glance at the river bend before jogging heavily to catch up to Nicholas, "What were you doing down there?"

Nicholas ignored him and Balushin began to lose his breath in his effort to keep pace with Nicholas.

The Russian men were assembled outside the officers' quarters. The dogs were lying languidly by the fire that had been rebuilt in the courtyard. An enormous black cauldron hung over the wood fire, belching bubbles of steam as it boiled. Nicholas recognized the fort's cook from the salmon feast the previous night. The aroma wafted through the courtyard. Nicholas' mouth watered and he understood why the hungry men were gathered eagerly around the fire. The chef had been chopping some vegetables for the stew on a roughly hewed timber that served as a makeshift table. He dropped the ingredients into the cauldron and mopped his brow before picking up the giant wooden spoon to stir.

He glanced up at the men and yelled loudly, "You won't get a bite until after the liturgy. Captain's ordered a fine Sunday meal for you, but you will have to wait. Get on with you."

One of the dogs snarled.

Igor stood from where he had been crouching next to the fire like an animal about to pounce on his prey. "Captain's orders," he scorned. "We are waiting for Captain's orders. So, don't get bossy with us, Cook."

Balushin barked a command to the men as Nicholas stepped into the officer's quarters. The aroma of the officer's meal hit him, and his stomach growled. Again, he recognized the Captain's cook from the ship, standing over the wood stove with an array of pans, hissing, boiling and steaming. Captain Zaikov, Konovalov, the priest, and every officer were assembled closely in the small area.

Zaikov greeted Nicholas warmly, "Ah, good, Nicholas. There you are. I was just telling the officers our plans for today and this week. Come. Have some coffee."

Nicholas accepted the tin cup from the cook, careful not to burn his hand or his mouth on the hot liquid. It was bitter and strong yet deliciously invigorating. He quickly learned that Balushin had forgotten to mention that Zaikov had meetings planned first for the officers and then the rest of the men. Zaikov commanded Konovalov to inform those officers for whom this was their first voyage to Cook Inlet of the sciences and practices necessary for maritime travel on the inlet. Konovalov, wan but otherwise recovered from his hangover and emotional meltdown, stood up to address the men who had arrived with Zaikov. As he opened his mouth to speak, there was a loud bang. The cook had opened the oven door of the wood stove, and using his apron, yanked out a baking pan of several round loaves of aromatic bread, which he deftly set on the table.

"Ah, prosphora," both the cook and the monk murmured in unison. The entire room erupted into laughter.

Zaikov addressed the priest, "Communion is ready." Father Iosaf nodded and smiled broadly.

Zaikov held his hand up and the men fell silent. He pointed to Konovalov to begin.

Konovalov cleared his throat. "These tides are the highest I have ever known. There is a bore tide with a rip tide wave of several feet and the current of a fast river. The inlet is covered with ashy silt from the volcanic eruptions through the past eons. It is like a slick clay or a snot."

He paused as the men snorted in amusement.

"In the fall, there are very high tides, up to thirty feet. The weather here is unpredictable, changing at a moment's notice. But the one thing you must be most careful of is the current. The river current is very strong, and the tidal current is deceptively strong." He elaborated on the way to get on and off the beach and follow the riverbed into the deeper water of the inlet, avoiding the treacherous and enormous rocks haphazardly strewn offshore or hidden by the tide.

Konovalov spoke of weather and seasons, the natives and local wildlife, the terrain and geography of the area in all directions. Finally, Zaikov stood and motioned for silence. He explained that he was picking a crew and sailing on the first favorable tide to the settlement across the inlet. He wanted to make sure everything was in order before the weather turned with the fast-approaching autumn, and to get an idea of the fur trade there. He would take Father Iosaf, who was certain that Father Juvenal was there.

The officers were told to line up outside the quarters while he addressed the men. They lumbered outside, each glancing back longingly at the food on the stove. Zaikov stood on the step of the quarters and addressed the men in the yard in a clear strong voice. He ordered that the men attend the Sunday service and a great feast would follow.

Briefly, Father Iosaf listened to the few men who desired confession. Then, the Sunday liturgy was held. Icons framed in gold were carefully set up in the tiny log structure that stood near the far end of the fort, above the wooded ravine of the creek that ran down to the beach. The door was left open so that the men could join the liturgy service while standing outside, since only the priest and four of the senior officers could stand inside. The tiny room had no windows or stove. The incense billowed out the door and rose in mystical clouds above the men outside. Father Iosaf intoned the rite solemnly. Nicholas shot a glance at

Konovalov and Balushin. Their heads were bowed, and he could not see their expressions to read what they were thinking. After the final blessing, the assembly of men moved to the cooking area and eagerly waited for the meal.

Large tables and benches of roughly hewed spruce trees were quickly set up in the middle of the yard. Men lined up with bowls past the cauldron of stew as the cook ladled a generous heaping in each. Mountains of biscuits and bread were piled in the center of each table. After the monk's blessing, the men attacked the food with gusto. Zaikov and the officers turned to the officers' quarters. The cook had opened the door and was fanning perspiration from his bright red face with his apron. The aroma of the food on the fully laden table made Nicholas' stomach growl.

The officers ate heartily, drinking liberally from the rare wine that Zaikov had brought. At first, the men ate with no time to speak between mouthfuls. Then, as the hunger turned to contentment, remarks about various events were made. Finally, as the wine was emptied and the vodka was poured, the conversation was animated. They talked of the success of the fur trade in the area surrounding the fort. They talked of the land and waterways in the area, as well as the mountains, especially those volcanoes that puffed and threatened to erupt. They talked of animals and the world's largest king salmon species that spawned up the Kenai River and compared the seasons with those of other places, including their native homeland of Russia. Zaikov gave the latest news of the Tsarina Catherine and the Russian political climate and governmental policies. The Tsarina was getting older and wanted to marry her granddaughter, Alexandra, to the King of Sweden. King Gustav IV of Sweden wanted his future wife to convert from Orthodoxy to Lutheranism in vain. When he arrived in Russia to meet his perspective bride, it was apparent she would not be converted from Orthodoxy as he demanded. He abruptly canceled the match and returned home to Sweden. Although the Tsarina had been a devout follower of Voltaire, reform in Russia was slow and difficult. Konovalov then talked of the English and Spanish explorers who had sailed into the inlet. Finally, the subject of the local native peoples arose. Nicholas noticed a subtle look of warning exchanged between Balushin and Konovalov whose lips had been loosened by the vodka. Nicholas caught the barely perceptible nod of Konovalov as he drunkenly acknowledged Balushin's silent warning.

In a voice full of reluctant admiration for his subject, Konovalov gave an account of what he had learned of the indigenous Kenaitze. Immediately, he and Balushin agreed heartily that the women were beautiful, and the race was wholesome and fair, more attractive than any other race the Russians had encountered in the Great Land of Alaska. Nicholas recalled Acts Quickly and he silently agreed. A strange stirring in his heart made him realize he was very curious about this famed beauty of the women which he wanted to see for himself. He began to listen more carefully. Konovalov described what he had ascertained of the culture and beliefs. The Denaina had a distinct and strong religion, they called the Spirit of Life *nilq'ech'*. Their God was called *Naqeltani*. They cremated their dead and believed that the spirit of the dead could haunt the living. They called belief in things that could not be seen *K'ech'Eltani*. The people who pursued this belief had roles. Konovalov spoke of the roles of the Shaman, Dreamer, Sky Reader, medical doctor, Prophet, and a powerful priest, which he didn't fully understand but hoped to learn more. He admired the language, though he knew little. Balushin joined in the conversation when it turned to the native practices of trapping, hunting, and harvesting resources from the land. They discussed the efficiency of the native technology in their home building, food preservation, tool making and clothing. Konovalov described the watercraft the natives used to hunt beluga in the inlet, the harpoons they used for killing seals, as well as nets and spears for the king, sockeye, pink and silver salmon that spawned in great numbers in the river.

The afternoon quickly turned to evening, and soon the cook was lighting candles in the room and serving a strong tea and cakes. Outside the quarters, the men still gathered, drinking, laughing, dancing and singing. Zaikov turned the conversation to the trading routes and travel to the nearby villages throughout the area. Slowly, an almost imperceptible change overcame the entire fort. Voices became edged with a tautness. The officers grew restless as the men fell quiet in the yard. Suddenly, the dogs began barking in a loud chorus and the door of the quarters opened, startling the men inside. The priest entered, his robes and beard flowing in a hushed rustling, like an apparition. The officers gaped a long moment in silence. The monk studied the men in return, his eyes and the crucifix on his chest glinting in the candlelight. Wood burning in the stove crackled like a gunshot, breaking the silence.

Zaikov, nonplussed, stood up. "Father Ioasaf. I thought you were here all this time. I didn't know you were outside. Where were you?" He motioned to the cook to bring a plate and to the officers to clear a spot for the religious man to join them at the table.

The monk sat down and casually stroked his beard. Nicholas thought he saw amusement in the priest's eyes. "I was talking with the native chief. He sent his son just after I blessed the food to ask me to come and bless the natives. So, I went."

He nodded thanks to the cook as a bowl of food was laid before him and a glass of wine found. The monk solemnly bowed his head, crossed himself and folded his long slim fingers in a brief prayer. The other men waited as if they were holding their breath.

As he finished and crossed himself again, Father Iosaf chuckled, "You all looked like you saw a ghost."

The monk's statement suspended in the air and the men in the log building became aware of the darkening evening outside the window. The ghost. No one had dared to think about it until now. The tension in the room was thick, like the fog that now hung off the bluff over the sands and the river mouth, muffling the sounds of the tide and driving the men outside in the yard to close and lock the fort doors before huddling together around the cooking fire. Wood was hastily gathered from the piles and thrown on the fire, while more wood was thrown within reach of the light given by the flames. They still drank vodka, but gone was the boisterous commotion of the sunny Sabbath afternoon, as they now hunched forward and conversed in hushed tones. The singing and dancing had faded away with the light. The dogs had retreated to their beds along the building walls, whining and growling. Steadily, a dark cutting chill invaded the fort, borne on the fog like a menacing heaviness threatening terror in the hearts of the Russians.

The monk, having blessed his plate now began consuming it hungrily.

Captain Zaikov stood up and stretched his arms as if to display his ease and fearlessness. "What of this 'ghost', Konovalov?"

"It is like a curse. We are haunted and we fear the devil himself," Balushin muttered under his breath.

Konovalov added in a trembling voice that cracked with fear, "The devil is a white specter. It screams curses at us. The wailing. It is Rusalka . . ." He broke off.

There were loud gasps. The men winced. Rusalka. The pale woman in a flowing white dress who appeared out of the sands and grasses along a river. She lured men into the river to drown. The souls of the men were imprisoned under the river currents in a cold wet hell of eternal dancing to Rusalka's songs.

"Pshaw," scoffed the priest, gazing up from his meal with

amusement. "You really believe it is Rusalka. The river has a ghost? An evil spirit?"

He waved his hand in dismissal. "Where is your faith?"

He wiped his mouth and continued, "Too bad it isn't the first week of June. I would hold a Rusalka Week and we could all put some garlic on, burn incense and dance around singing chants. Then, the river would be safe to swim in again." The monk glared around the room. "Superstitious fools . . ."

"Yes. What is this 'ghost'?" Zaikov wanted to know.

His brow was furrowed. Nicholas knew the Captain had been displeased with the condition of the men and the fort when he arrived the day before. He knew the tight ship Zaikov ran and how little disobedience he tolerated from his men. The notion that the fort was haunted and that a white apparition screeched at the men from across the river in the shadows of the night would be utter nonsense to Zaikov. As Nicholas eyed the Captain, he saw a wave of fury flash across his face as he glared at Konovalov. The fort commander was pale and shivering.

At first, Konovalov's voice was again faint and quivering, but he attempted to muster his composure.

"Captain, I do not know what to say. I have seen the ghost myself. It shows itself as a wraith in white just across the river. It shrieks . . . oh God . . . .how it shrieks. You can hear it scream all the way up here at the fort, carried on the wind. Then, it disappears into the sand and grass. Amos is right. It is a devil. Every time it appears, something bad happens. Then sickness comes to the men, and they become injured or begin to argue and fight. Men have fallen in the river and drowned. Food spoils. Storms rise. Hell, one time a great brown bear came and destroyed our cache of fish stored for the winter. It killed two of our dogs and mauled a man before we shot it. The furs have become damaged by the rodents or damp. Yes, I believe we are cursed."

Nicholas and the other officers stirred restlessly. The cloud of dread and fear hanging from Konovalov's words made them squirm and they felt far from home. Horrible images of demons danced in their imaginations. Storybook pictures of the evil spirit Rusalka from their childhoods were brought to their minds unbidden. They looked at Zaikov. He was listening, his eyes narrowed.

"You will see, Captain," Balushin said. "It will come, maybe tonight. You go to the bluff, and you will see."

"There are no ghosts. Rusalka is a silly children's tale told by lowly ignorant farmers and midwives. There are no demons," Zaikov returned. "It must be some beluga or other animal. What about the natives? What do they say?"

"They refuse to talk about it," Konovalov answered. "They only say that it wasn't here before we built the fort."

"Are you sure it isn't one of them?" Zaikov asked.

"Yes," Konovalov explained. "They say that side of the river is where a village stood a long time ago. They stay away from there. They say it is the sacred ground of their ancestors."

Nicholas recalled the mysterious apparition he himself had witnessed the night before and spoke. "Even so, Officer Konovalov, maybe someone is playing a trick on us."

He turned to Zaikov. "Father Ioasaf and I saw a light last night on the far shore. It disappeared into the fog. I could not make out what it was. Whatever it is, Captain, it sure frightens the men."

"I saw it too, Captain," Father Ioasaf joined in. "It moved like a human being with a light. Not a ghost. And even if it is Rusalka or some diabolical disembodied spirit, our Good Lord will protect us, now that the liturgy is being offered here."

Zaikov rubbed his eyes and sat down with a long sigh. The officers waited for his word. "Tomorrow, on the tide, we sail to Tyonek, fog or not."

He appointed two of the officers who had just arrived with him on the vessel to be in charge of the fort in his absence. Nicholas, along with the two senior officers, the fort cook, a handful of men from the ship and the nearly two hundred men already there would be left to hold it. Balushin, the monk and the majority of the men from the St. George were going with Zaikov.

There was a sharp rap at the door as the dogs began barking loudly. The officers, except Zaikov and the monk, jumped in alarm. Zaikov barked a command. The door flung open. It was Igor, his immense frame filling the door. His eyes bulged and his nose flared in fear.

"It is the ghost. Rusalka. She screams." The giant looked like a frightened child, quivering and whimpering.

Zaikov rose and gestured for the monk to accompany him. He strode to the door, grabbing his coat from the nail it was hanging on. He strung a belt with his pistol and sword around his hips before he snapped his fingers for an officer to bring a light. An officer and Nicholas brought lanterns as they joined the Captain out of the door. The men were tightly packed around the doors of the quarters, while the dogs barked and howled. Zaikov and Father Ioasaf froze in mid stride from the door as a scream pierced the night air on the icy breeze. Nicholas' blood ran cold. The shriek wailed and faded. Dogs whimpered and hid under steps and in corners.

Zaikov sprang into action. He grabbed the lantern from the officer and led the way to the fort entrance. Nicholas held his lantern high as he hurried to follow. Two men opened the door and the men jammed behind Zaikov as he stepped out. It was pitch black. The air was thick with icy fog. All hint of the warm autumn evening had been lost in the frigid air. Zaikov led the way down the path to the top of the bluff with Father Ioasaf at his heels, his black robes rustling as he hurried. Nicholas followed the monk, holding the lantern high so the men behind him could see the path. Zaikov paused where the path began its descent to the beach, and peered into the inky blackness.

The fog was impenetrable and icy cold. Nicholas stood beside him. The two lanterns cast a feeble light several feet into the fog. Another scream rose on a gust of wind. It was fainter as if the ghost was moving south along the beach. Then, all fell silent, save the wind. The gusts seemed to billow the fog, which began to strengthen as if stirred to a tempest by the screams. The dark, ominous gusts seemed to attack the men, as if angered by the lanterns that pierced its void.

Zaikov snorted and turned back to the fort.

At the door of the quarters, he addressed the men huddled at his heels. "The gate is shut and locked. Father Ioasaf is with us. You have nothing to fear. Rusalka is an old wives' tale. Nothing more. There are no ghosts. Get some sleep, men. We sail tomorrow early on the tide."

The Captain turned and went inside. Despite his words, an air of dread hung over the fort. Each man fell silent, keeping his fears to himself as he retired for the night. Outside in the courtyard, the night watchmen sat silently by the fire without speaking to one another, each straining to listen, but for what they did not know.

SIX

FEAR HAS BIG EYES. NICHOLAS LAY AWAKE under the stairway, staring into the blackness of the officers' quarters. He could hear the officers' snores from the second level between gusts of wind. The wind was like a wild beast outside, alternating between violent charges and hissing, sneaky attempts to get inside. He could hear the gusts coming up over the bluff and smashing into the fort's walls and sides of the officers' quarters, causing the windows to shudder. When the gust had exhausted its slamming effort, a wheezing breeze slithered through the courtyard and slipped in between the logs of the building, finding every missing chink and warped opening to enter in and expel its icy breath inside. Nicholas pulled the furs tighter around him. He was still fully dressed, as he had only removed his boots to lie down. His knife and pistols were at the ready. Unbidden thoughts plagued him.

He saw Acts Quickly's face. The spirits. Haunting. Strange non-Christian dreamers, prophets and shamen. Burning corpses. The unholy screams piercing the air from across the river. Pictures of

Rusalka from a children's book. An uncontrollable desire to see the beauty of the native women. Nicholas lay in his bed under the stairs and closed his eyes.

He steered his thoughts to the story of Rusalka. The first time he had heard the fairy tale was when he was a very small child in the arms of his mother. He tried to recall how she smelled, how she had felt as she wrapped her arms around him and softly told the story, laying in his trundle bed after he had clamored for a scary bedtime story.

"Once upon a time, a long, long time ago, there was a young princess. She was very, very, very beautiful. She lived in a grand palace with her father, the king, and her mother, the queen. The palace had a spacious garden with an orchard of many fruit trees, such as different kinds of apple trees. At the edge of the garden was a large river that ran through the entire kingdom from the cold mountains in the north to the warm sea in the south. The princess loved to walk through the orchard and garden to sit by the bank of the river. Her long hair flowed to about her shoulders and her beautiful dress was spread around her on the grass where she sat. As she watched the ducks swim by on the river, she would sing a song. She sang a lovely song about her dream of one day marrying a fine prince and going to his palace. There she sat on the green grassy bank of the river, singing, until her mother sent the maid to tell the princess to come back to the palace before evening.

"One day, the princess was singing her song about her dream of marrying a prince when a boat came floating by on the river. There in the boat was a handsome prince. He landed his boat on the grassy bank where the princess sat. He told her that he had heard her singing and wanted to know who was singing such a beautiful song. The handsome prince was from the next kingdom up the river. The princess invited him to her palace to meet her father and mother and join them for dinner. The prince gladly accepted her

offer and took her hand to help her up. They walked through the orchard back to the palace. The king was pleased to meet the prince, and the queen invited him to eat dinner with them and spend the night before continuing on the river in his boat. The prince was happy to accept. Meanwhile, the princess had fallen in love. As she prepared for dinner, she put on her finest dress and had her maid braid her long hair before putting a jeweled tiara on her head. The princess spoke incessantly of how wonderful the prince was and how she hoped that he was the man she would marry and live with happily ever after.

"The prince enjoyed his dinner. He listened politely as the king told him about his kingdom. He listened politely as the queen told him about her orchards. He listened politely as the princess told him about how she loved to sit on the riverbank and sing songs. He slept in the palace that night. The next morning, he told the king that he must go home or his father, the king of the next kingdom which was up the river, would send soldiers to look for him. 'But, before I go, I must tell you that I have fallen in love with your daughter and wish to marry her,' said the prince. The king called for his daughter and asked her if she wanted to accept the prince's hand in marriage and be the future queen of the next kingdom. She was delighted and accepted the offer to marry the prince. The king and queen were pleased, and the four of them discussed plans for a wedding. It was decided that the week after the next that the prince would return to marry the princess and take her as his wife to his kingdom up the river where she would meet his father, his mother, and all the royal household. Then, the prince said he must go. The king and queen bade farewell to the prince. The princess and her maid walked with the prince through the garden and orchard to the riverbank where his boat was tied. The prince promised to return in two weeks to marry the princess, and she stood on the grassy bank watching him paddle his boat up the river until he was out of sight. The next two weeks were busy, busy, busy. The palace was decorated. The wedding banquet was prepared. An exquisite wedding dress for the princes was sewn by the royal seamstress. Invitations were sent to guests far and wide for the wedding. The princess was the king and queen's only child, and so they spared no expense for her wedding.

"Finally, the day before the wedding arrived. The princess and her maid went to the green grassy bank of the river and waited. The prince came around the bend of the river in his boat looking ever so handsome. He was taken to the palace and given a room to spend the night before his wedding to the princess.

"The next morning, the princess woke early full of excitement for her wedding. She put the wedding dress on by herself and brushed her long hair before setting her wedding veil on her head. She waited. When it was time for the ceremony, a servant was sent to look for the prince in his room. He was gone.

"The king came to his daughter as she sat in her wedding dress in her chamber with the sad news. He held a letter in his hand. It said: I am sorry, but I cannot marry your daughter. It is her maid who I am in love with. The maid is returning with me to my kingdom, where she will become my wife.

'No!' the princess screamed. She picked up the skirts of her exquisite white wedding dress and ran through the garden and orchard to the green grassy bank of the river. She intended to stop the prince before he left in his boat to return to his kingdom up the river and beg him to marry her. She would banish the maid to the wild forests beyond so she would never be seen again. But the boat was gone. The prince was gone. The maid was gone.

With a loud shriek, the princess cast herself off the riverbank. The exquisite wedding dress and long wedding veil grew heavy in the water and pulled the princess down, down, down into the dark river water, where she drowned.

The king and queen both died of a broken heart. The kingdom felt abandoned. Wild thorns grew and entangled the orchard and garden. Wild beasts roamed the desolate kingdom. The land became a dark, cold place where travelers hurried through and dreaded passing along the river. At night, the terrifying specter of a pale thin woman in a ragged white dress with long tendrils of hair would crawl from the river. She screamed and shrieked, and the blood ran cold of all who heard her. She sought men and lured them to their drowning death in the watery grave under the river. Woe to the men who heard and saw the ghost in white along the river at night. She bade them dance a wedding dance for all eternity. Rusalka. The unclean spirit of the vengeful princess who suffered the jilting by her beloved prince on her wedding day."

When he heard this, Little Nicholas had felt tears of terror well up in his eyes. His mother clucked her tongue as she caressed his cheek and kissed his forehead.

As she wiped the tears, she chided him for asking for a scary bedtime story. *"Fear has big eyes,"* she laughed, while gently tweaking his tiny nose.

She continued, "That means that if you want to be scared, you will go around looking for something to be frightened of. There is nothing to be frightened of. Rusalka is a silly fairy tale told to scare children and warn men about mistreating women, Nicholas. That is all the story is. A story. Now, close your eyes and sleep."

His mother had made a cross on his forehead, kissed him one last time and turned out the light as she left the room.

Nicholas snorted. He had believed his mother when she said the story of Rusalka was a silly fairy tale, and as a young child had dismissed the fear it evoked from his mind during that night long ago. Now, he was disgusted that the rough full grown company men of the fort were frightened by a mere fairy tale. It made no sense if a grown man of reason thought about it. Why would Rusalka be here in Kenay? Why would she haunt the Russians at the fort when none of the men were princes? Nicholas concluded the entire affair was nonsense, and he turned his face to the wall and struggled to get to sleep. After some uncomfortably long hours, he fell into an uneasy slumber of dark dreams.

Fear has big eyes. An ugly voice snarled the words of the old Russian proverb. Nicholas snapped awake in an instant with his hand on his pistol. The heaviness of the dark made him gasp for breath. His heart drummed loudly in his ears. Where had the voice come from? He was sure it was from the middle of the room by the table. Who was trying to scare him? Fury welled up in him at the thought of being taunted awake. He squinted into the darkness, barely moving his head so that it would appear he was still sleeping, thereby giving him the advantage of observing the voice without it knowing he was awake. A long moment passed. He could see and hear nothing. Something still nagged him. What was it? Then, he realized the wind had fallen silent. His ears and eyes strained. Nothing. Had he dreamed of the voice? He waited long minutes. Nothing. Suddenly, the air in the room was stuffy and the furs covering him were suffocating and hot. He threw them back and stepped silently into his boots. He grabbed his coat and slipped outside, quietly shutting the door behind him.

He stood a moment in surprise. The bitter chill of the earlier evening had warmed to a pleasant fresh sweetness, like a balm that washed his tensions away. The night watch men's fire was cheery and bright, illuminating everything, even the edges of the courtyard. Nicholas chuckled lightly as he spied the two forms of the watchmen, wrapped tightly in their furs and dreaming peacefully next to the fire. He looked around and to his surprise, the door of the fort was slightly ajar. He stepped forward, consumed with curiosity and strangely unafraid.

A peculiar sound reached his ears from overhead. He paused. Was it a voice? He looked up. It took him a moment to comprehend what he was seeing and hearing. It appeared to be a raven swooping low over the fort. The sky was black, and he could see lighter gray edges of heavy clouds weighing down above, the front of a terrifyingly massive storm system moving in from the west over the fort. Yet, he was still not afraid. Curiosity burned within him. He walked to the door of the fort and peered down the trail to the bluff. It took a moment for his eyes to adjust.

A tall figure stood on the trail about fifty feet away with its back turned to him. He stared, frozen, aware that he was in the doorway between safety and a great, unfathomable world outside. He wondered whether he would be safe from the unknown figure if he yelled and shut the door. Suddenly, the figure turned, slowly as if on a pedestal. It was Acts Quickly. As the young Denaina man turned, he spoke in his Denaina language words that Nicholas oddly understood to be role titles. It was as if Acts Quickly had four sides and four faces that showed as he spun in four rotations. Dreamer. Prophet. Sky Reader. Priest. Nicholas stirred, conscious that more ravens were circling over the fort in the dark now and more strange, voice-like sounds were coming down.

Then, a light caught the corner of the Russian's eye. It streamed from behind him in the fort and through the doorway of the shack that had been built for the Orthodox monks. As he studied it, it grew in brightness. He began to walk towards it across the courtyard. The beams swelled up and the ravens, the storm, and the dark figure vanished from his thought. He wanted to see what was in the shack that was emitting such a lovely light, for he was drawn to it like a moth to a candle. At the doorway, the luminescence was great, but it did not hurt his eyes. He strained to make out what was there. A woman stood in the middle of the shack. She was dressed in a pure white dress and a magnificent white fur cloak trimmed in ermine tails. While veiled from view with her back to him, he sensed great beauty and a desire to see and understand her possessed him. He stepped towards her eagerly. She looked to her left.

As Nicholas advanced, the little shack opened up, becoming the great palace of the Tsarina Catherine in St. Petersburg. There. The royal head of all Russia, Catherine the Great, herself sat. She was looking at the woman in the white dress. He paused. Dimly, he understood the Tsarina was demanding the white furs. No. Something was wrong. She was demanding the execution of the beautiful woman.

Nicholas jerked awake.

The cook was in the kitchen area in the graying gloom of pre-dawn. He had dropped the pot for heating water for tea and coffee. He swore under his breath, darting an apologetic glance at Nicholas and grimacing. He quickly filled the pot with water from the barrel in the corner and set it on the stove. Then, the cook began to light the fire in the cook stove.

Nicholas rubbed his eyes, struggling to clear his head. The dream had seemed so real. He sat up and shook off the sleep. He was angry with himself. Even as a child, he did not believe in scary stories of Rusalka or other ghosts. He did not fear spirits or curses. He was not superstitious and never had any tendency towards the supernatural. He was practical, reasoned, studied and clear headed. Nicholas pulled his boots on and realized he did not like Fort Kenay. It was a disturbed place. It began to occur to him that if there was a curse on the redoubt, the blame lay on Konovalov and Balushin. What had they done?

At that moment, Captain Zaikov and Father Ioasaf drowsily descended the stairway. Nicholas joined them at the table. When the strong hot coffee was served, they began to discuss the plan for the journey.

Zaikov spoke with disgust, "Konovalov has taken to his bed. He claims he is too ill to go with us to Tyonek and instead sends Balushin. Balushin says he is worried about Konovalov and insists that Igor stay to take care of Konovalov. So, keep a close eye on those two, Nicholas. I am leaving Demidov and Vasilev to fix things up around the fort and start building the new church."

Nicholas waited until Father Ioasaf had left the officers' quarters for the shack to pray with the icons before he approached the Captain.

"Captain, the atmosphere of this place is severely disturbing. I sense a darkness here. I don't know what Konovalov and Balushin have done, but an evil cloud is over this fort. Something bad either has happened or will happen. Take me with you. I want to return to Russia." Zaikov surveyed him curiously.

Nicholas added, "There is nothing here but chaos and ill will. You see for yourself what a filthy dump this fort is."

"So, you haven't found what you were commissioned here to find?" Zaikov spoke with faint amusement.

He looked at the young officer, whose cheeks were flushed and his jaw clenched. He knew Nicholas was not affected by the ghost with superstition and could see Nicholas was not speaking out of fear, but he still wasn't sure what was going on in the young man's mind. He drained his coffee robustly in one gulp.

"Alaska. It will grow on you even if you don't love her at first sight. She is a fresh start for any Russian willing to work hard to make his fortune. Then, a young man can return home rich and settle down. Unless he prefers the wilderness and builds his own empire here." He could see his words had no effect on Nicholas, for the young officer's mind was made up.

The Captain considered the matter carefully. When the St. George's Captain had been approached by a wealthy man in St. Petersburg, he hadn't asked any questions about allowing Nicholas as a fresh officer on his crew. Many rubles had silenced questions. Someone very rich and extremely powerful had wanted the young man to sail to Fort Kenay. He had accepted the rubles with a certain interest in seeing what Nicholas' sponsor had wanted done once they had arrived at the fort. However, now that the Russians had arrived at the Alaskan fort, the situation was a terrible mess.

Konovalov himself was irrational and displayed signs of lunacy and hysteria. How could he and Balushin have prepared for the coming winter to trade for furs from the natives when there was such superstition of a ghost among the men at the fort? Zaikov reflected further. What would his superiors say if he left as soon as he arrived because a young rich officer was homesick? They would want to know where the shipload of furs was that they paid him to sail to Alaska to obtain. Yet, he also needed to deliver his findings back to his superiors that Konovalov should be replaced immediately as commander of the fort. If he left within a month, he could return to Russia before the winter storms blew.

"I need you here at the fort while I take Father Ioasaf across the inlet. I was told by your commissioner that what you needed to do was only in Kenay. He insisted that you arrive here and be allowed to carry out your mission. So, there is no need for you to sail with me to Tyonek across the inlet. We will come back and talk about this again. It is only for a week or two at the most. Konovalov says there is a load of furs there, so I will need men with me. Then I will return here, pick you up and make sure Konovalov is settled for the winter, and we will sail back to Russia before the winter storms begin."

Zaikov continued, "If you are sure that you have accomplished what you came here for, you will be on the St. George sailing home."

Nicholas was silent. The men upstairs began stirring as they smelled the coffee and breakfast cooking. Soon, they stomped heavily down the rough stairs and the kitchen was filled with hungry, boisterous men who were looking forward to the sailing across the inlet, away from the ominous atmosphere of the fort.

The breakfast was hearty and hurried. The cook was eager to pack for the trip and enlisted Balushin to wash the dishes and tidy up the kitchen. Nicholas subtly surveyed Balushin to see if he could discover any clue to the mystery of the screaming ghost or why the men claimed the fort was cursed. But he found no clues to the mystery in the conniving wretch's behavior. The man was as cheerful and eager to sail as the rest of the men. Konovalov remained in his bed upstairs while Igor sat sullenly in the corner of the yard with the dogs.

As the men prepared to leave, Father Ioasaf pulled Nicholas aside and tugged his arm, steering him to the shack that served as the church. He looked over his shoulder as he led the way inside the small hut out of sight. Once inside, after shutting the makeshift door, he blessed him with his gold cross, touching it to his forehead, murmuring a hurried prayer for protection.

The old cleric met Nicholas' eyes and whispered, laying a hand on his arm, "*My son, be safe.* Be careful and watch your back. Don't go out alone. Don't trust any of the men who serve Konovalov here or who Zaikov leaves behind at the fort. Avoid Igor. That man is a brute. Stay away from Konovalov too. He seems crazy. Only fraternize with the officers from the St. George who are staying and the men who sailed with us from Russia."

He paused a second as he searched Nicholas' face. The monk was pleading his warning. Nicholas opened his mouth to tell the priest to not be concerned on his account, since he was well trained in all forms of combat, and armed and capable of protecting himself.

Father Ioasaf held a hand up, cutting him off. "I think you can trust the Denaina chief and his son. But don't be seen getting too friendly with them or you will be under suspicion by Konovalov and his watchdog, Igor." He released Nicholas' arm, stepped back and sighed deeply.

"The chief told me why Father Juvenal isn't here. He told me that the natives welcomed Father Juvenal, but they don't trust Konovalov and Balushin. The native leader fears something bad has happened. He is deeply troubled about his daughter and Father Juvenal is missing. He thinks Father went to Tyonek to get away from trouble. He told me that if I don't find Father Juvenal in Tyonek, I am to go back to him, and he will tell me everything that has happened. See, Nicholas . . . I think Father Juvenal knows something about this so-called ghost and curse. He knows what Konovalov and Balushin did. If I can find him, I can solve this mystery . . . but I fear . . ." The monk started at a sharp rap on the door and the rattling as if someone was trying to yank it open.

The two men turned and through the cracks of the poorly cut slats of the door, they saw Balushin.

Father Ioasaf closed his eyes and began praying loudly as Balushin yanked the door open.

The monk stopped and opened his eyes wide, as if he was surprised by the stout man's entrance.

"Amos. My son. Are you here for confession, too? Quickly now. Quickly, son. We want to get going. Can't keep Captain Zaikov waiting, can we now?"

He steered Nicholas out of the shack. "Your sins are forgiven, son. Go and sin no more." He turned to Balushin. Amos Balushin's cheeks were burning bright, and he uttered a low growl as Nicholas pushed by him. He muttered something about being sent to get the priest.

Father Ioasaf laughed cheerfully and slapped Balushin on the back. "We better go then."

SEVEN

NICHOLAS STOOD AT THE TOP OF THE BLUFF trail with his arms folded across his chest. The sails of St. George the Victorious billowed white far beyond the mud shallows of the inlet. The last load of men were rowing the skiff from the beach below the bluff to the ship. One of the rowing crew looked back at the shores and up to the bluff top. He thought the figure was a sturdy tree, before realizing it was the young officer. Two fellow officers from the St. George, Demidov and Vasilev, had remained with Nicholas. They were middle aged, refined and reserved, yet Nicholas did not doubt their capabilities nor their strong leadership over the rough men in their charge. The officers were almost as tall as Nicholas, broad shouldered and muscular. They had fought wars for their empire in foreign lands and knew well how to protect themselves and command rough men.

Vasilev stood behind Nicholas and spoke with resolve, "Well, we will keep the fort until the Captain returns. It looks like Konovalov will be in his bed for the duration. He claims an ulcer or some such nonsense. We should have firewood and plenty of supplies to get us through the next couple of weeks, so if need be, we don't have to venture far from the fort. I am sure the Captain will return on time."

Demidov smoothed his beard and grinned. He touched a gold crucifix that hung around his neck over his immaculate uniform and leaned close in a conspiring manner. "I do not believe in old tales. I do not fear Rusalka or any ghosts."

Vasilev swung his long arms across the shoulders of Demidov and Nicholas. "Maybe we can have a look see at the truth of all this talk about the beautiful women down in the village." He grinned at Demidov and thumped Nicholas' back.

"Dear Officer Demidov, you and I have lovely wives waiting at home, but maybe we can play uncles and find our boy Nicholas a beautiful wife here."

Demidov roared at the deep color of Nicholas' cheeks, adding, "Now there's a happy fairy tale. Love found on the blue river of Alaska. And they can live happily ever after in Kenay."

They all chuckled as Nicholas shook his head. The three men left the bluff and returned to the quarters. The sky was still gray, yet the winds remained calm, adding to the heaviness of the air. The outgoing tide had been one of the particularly high autumnal inflows which Nicholas guessed to be near thirty feet. Over the river flats beyond, gulls and eagles cried in hungry pleas.

The three officers of the St. George immediately organized the duties of the nearly two hundred men under their charge at the redoubt. Every man whom Zaikov had left behind set to work on the fort. Igor was quiet now that he was alone and obeyed the orders with his enormous head hung. Demidov suggested that the first task was to improve the fortification of the fort. Dried spruce timbers piled on the north side of the fort were hauled inside and cut into rough slats. The walls of the fort and the buildings were repaired. Demidov, Vasilev and Nicholas led the work hauling, sawing, and hammering.

The officers were fit and strong, so their men worked alongside them in admiration and eagerness to show their cooperation. Demidov and Vasilev shared with Nicholas what their orders were. Zaikov wanted the redoubt to be strengthened and impenetrable. Then, he insisted that a log church be erected for the monks adjacent to the fort on the north side. Father Iosaf had brought gold coins to pay for a mission to be built near the redoubt, with quarters for more monks and possibly a school. He brought a deed from the company granting the mission property on the side of the creek ravine, at the edge of the flat land the fort was on. There was much work to be done before the seasons changed, and the snows of winter would begin to fall. In his absence, Zaikov wanted his men to get a solid two weeks start on the improvements to the redoubt.

The men worked until the sunset. The fort cook had prepared a hearty meal both for the officers and men with fresh cabbage and meat. The officers washed up and checked on Konovalov, who still lay on his bed, pale and quiet. He murmured that he needed to rest longer. Demidov shook his head and led the way downstairs to the waiting meal.

Nicholas enjoyed the food and company. Demidov and Vasilev were talkative and shared amusing anecdotes of their wives and children. Demidov had four children, three sons and a daughter. Vasilev had only two daughters. Of the officers, Demidov had spent the most time at the royal court in St. Petersburg. He spoke of the great celebrations of royal members with feasts and balls. His family had been prominent since the days of Tsar Peter the Great. Nicholas listened quietly, picturing the scenes in his mind. He did not wonder why these two men were now hard at work laboring intensely in the remote wilderness of Alaska. He knew it was the lucrative pay that the company offered these expert ship-men which drew them. They both longed to buy their own estates and provide the best schooling for their children.

After dinner, the conversation turned to sailing as a bottle of vodka was opened and shot glasses were distributed by the cook. Demidov had just begun a discourse on the early Russian explor-ers, beginning with Gregory Shelikhov, when there was a tap at the door. The officers paused as the cook opened the door.

There stood Igor and four Denaina men. "They want to speak to the new commander of the fort," Igor grumbled. The officers looked at each other and back at the Denaina men. There was an older man who stood erect and proud. He was flanked by three young men who were eying the officers curiously. Nicholas recognized Acts Quickly and realized that the old man was the young Denaina's father, who was also the chief.

"Let them in," said Vasilev. "Do they understand Russian?"

To the officers' utter surprise, the chief spoke in heavily accented but conversational Russian. "I am Qeshqa, or Chief of the Shk'ituk't."

Vasilev waved the group towards seats around the table. He ordered the cook to make tea and serve biscuits.

Acts Quickly introduced the two young men as Spear and Last Waters, his cousins and nephews of the Chief. Nicholas studied the cousins in the lantern light. Spear was dark and had an air of tense-ness around him, as if he were a coil ready to spring into action at any moment. Last Waters was fair, tall like his cousin and wore a faint expression of boredom. Nicholas wondered if Last Waters had a wife or young woman that he would rather be keeping com-pany with that evening.

Nicholas admired the chief's etiquette in his speech and manner as he sat looking solemnly at the officers. Demidov explained that Konovalov was still the commander of the fort and how they were Zaikov's officers. He pointed out that Zaikov and the others had gone to Tyonek in search of Father Juvenal and to pick up a load of furs. He explained that the crew of the St. George planned to return to Russia before winter. The Denaina men listened intently. The chief asked about the mission. Demidov again explained that he and the men remaining in the fort planned to start work on the church after they fortified the redoubt. He asked the chief if the Denaina had furs ready to trade so Zaikov could bring them back to Russia. The chief answered that they did have a great deal of furs from sea otter and seals. The furs of wolves and beavers would be harvested over the winter and ready for the spring. The chief then asked whether Konovalov had joined Zaikov in sailing to Tyonek. He listened somberly as Demidov explained that Konovalov was upstairs at the moment, but too sick to join the other officers. The chief was concerned and asked what kind of sickness the man had. He had heard of deadly diseases that the Russians had brought to natives on the Aleutian Islands. Demidov assured him that it was from drinking too much vodka.

He added wryly, "Konovalov does seem pretty unsettled by this white ghost that screeches and wails on the sandbars of the river at night."

The chief responded, "The actions of humans in a place can leave a stench. The stench can attract bad spirits. Maybe it is this stench or a bad spirit that makes Konovalov sick."

Demidov shook his head. "Nyet. It is too much vodka. We will give the man a few days and then he will be back to work."

The conversation paused a moment as the men drank their tea. The cook replenished their cups and a plate of biscuits before going outside to collect supplies for the wood cook stove to use at breakfast.

Then, the chief smiled and spoke. "I will tell sukdu. A story."

Acts Quickly added, "Some of the story might not sound the same in Russian as it does in our language, but you can understand most of it."

The Russians listened politely in faint amusement. Demidov began to wonder how the Russians could persuade the natives to do most of the hard labor around the fort for them.

"A long time ago, before the Russians came, there was a village on the other side of the river. It was smaller than our village now. The villagers were simple and hardworking. They worked through all summer and fall to gather food for the long cold winter. They went into the brush and cut many poles. The poles were carried down to the river to construct a fish trap. Then, the villagers cut more poles and these were used to build drying wracks to hang salmon on. The salmon came. They swam into the fish trap. Some men took long sturdy spears to stab the fish out of the trap. Others had collected spruce roots and wove them into large baskets. They took the sinew from a caribou or moose and secured the nets onto large hoops. Then, long handles were bound onto the hoops, so that they fashioned a dip net. The men used these nets to dip the salmon out of the trap. We still use spears and dip nets as you have seen. Our fish trap is on the river above the village where the channel divides into two braids of water. The women and elderly would take the fish and cut them carefully. The cut fish was hung on the racks to dry. Young Denaina gathered dry wood and tended the fires that smoldered under the racks to keep the flies away from the fresh fish meat. The dried fish was taken down, cut into strips, dried again before being taken down and carefully stored in baskets. The baskets were made in the wintertime. Some were woven from the hearty grasses you see growing along the edge of the dunes of the beaches. Women gathered these grasses in the early fall and dried them in the corner of the house so that they could weave them into watertight baskets during the long cold dark winter months. Other baskets are made from birch bark.

The bark is cut in long strips from the live trees in a way that does not kill the tree. The bark pieces are soaked and then bent into the shape of a basket and sewn together at the seams with peeled spruce roots. The seams are folded in a specific way so that these baskets are also air and watertight. These ways have been handed down since the Coming of the Campfire People.

"One day in the fall, just like the season we are in now, the villagers were all done putting up the salmon. They also put-up berries, caribou and moose. They were getting ready to go hunting for seals. The village dogs began to bark. Then, out of the willows on the upriver side of the village, a giant walked on to the sandbar. He was as tall as a black spruce tree and heavyset, with a thick black beard and hair that hung down to his shoulders. His large face had course features and was frightening to look at, especially since his eyes were black. He lumbered heavily to the village. Men rushed to get their bows and spears. The chief stepped forward and asked the giant who he was. The giant just said he was hungry. He said he was so hungry he couldn't talk.

"So, the chief bade the giant to sit down at the edge of the village where a large driftwood log lay on the sand. The giant sat, resting his back against the log. The villagers disappeared into their houses, as if they were gathering a feast to lay before the giant. The chief assembled his finest warriors and whispered a plan to them. The men took knives and crept around the back of the driftwood log. Then, all at once, the men jumped on the log and stabbed the giant in the back of his head, neck and back. The giant was caught off guard and died quickly.

"The men cut the giant up and burned the body in a great bonfire." The chief paused and studied the reaction of the Russians.

Demidov and Vasilev chuckled nervously but their humor died in their throat after looking around at Acts Quickly and the others' solemn faces.

Vasilev cleared his throat and spoke. "That is quite a story. The poor giant. He was murdered for being hungry. We will have to keep an eye on dear Igor. He might be mistaken for your ugly giant. We need him around to do heavy work. I don't suppose you have a story for the wailing ghost, do you? I rather think it is belyj or beluga since I don't believe in ghosts. The sailors tell stories of the white whales that sing and wail quite eerily on the seas. Do you have beluga here in this area?"

The Denaina men nodded. The chief answered, "The qunshi have come back to the river. Spear saw one yesterday. What you call beluga, they come up the river to eat nudlaghi, the silver salmon. We came to invite you to watch our men hunt the nudlaghi tomorrow. Come and watch and then join us in the feast."

Demidov and Vasilev were hesitant.

The chief urged them, "We invited Konovalov and he came. He brings all the men of the fort and they eat. They bring some whale meat back for the winter. Come tomorrow."

Vasilev decided in response, "We got a lot of work done today. The extra meat for the fort's winter larders might not be a bad idea. I tell you what, Qeshqa, we will continue working on the fort because our company commander, Zaikov ordered us to get these tasks done while he is gone. We will send Nicholas. He can watch and then bring back the meat for our men to feast on and put up for the winter."

The chief seemed satisfied with the decision.

Demidov cleared his throat. He leaned back in his chair and viewed the chief through narrowed eyes. "I have a story for you, Qeshqa. It is a fine Russian story. I heard it when I just a young boy."

He glanced around the table. "In fact, I am sure all the men here were told this story when they were young boys."

Demidov smiled broadly. "*My story isn't about a giant. It is about a young man, Ivan Tsarevich. He was the youngest son of the* tsar. *As you know, what you call Qeshqa, we call tsar. The tsar had three sons. Ivan was the youngest. The older sons were simple and rather lazy. Now, the tsar had a lovely garden with a fine orchard in it. The orchard had many of the most succulent fruit trees growing there. Of all the trees in the orchard, the tsar treasured one on which golden apples grew. The apples were the finest of all the apples. They were sweet and crunchy and crisp. Every day, the tsar would stroll through his garden into the orchard. He would go to his prized apple tree and count the golden apples that grew on it before selecting the perfect one to enjoy. At first, the tsar just watched the apple tree blossom, then watched the blossoms turn into apples and then he waited for the apples to ripen to perfection. The golden apples meant everything to the tsar. The apples were so important to the tsar that he ordered guards to watch over the tree as it blossomed and bore fruit. The time came when the apples began to ripen to perfection, and the tsar went to count the apples. He was eager to find the first ripe apple so he could enjoy it with his meal. But to his horror, there was one less apple on the tree than the day before. The Tsar stood there in the orchard, recounting the apples until he was sure he hadn't made a mistake. An apple was missing. The tsar angrily called the guards and demanded to know where the missing apple was. The guards hung their heads. "The fire bird came and stole the apple."*

"The tsar believed his trusted guards. He knew that only the fire bird was cunning and daring enough to enter his orchard and steal the first golden apple that ripened to perfection. The tsar summoned his two oldest sons. "Catch the fire bird and bring it to me. In return, I will give whichever one of you brings me the fire bird half of my kingdom," he promised his sons. The sons hurried back to devise traps in which to catch the fire bird that night. Unfortunately, night after night, the fire bird stole the golden apple that ripened that day to perfection and foiled every trap the two older sons devised to catch

it. The king was very upset. Ivan went to his father, the tsar, and begged him to let him try. Desperate to catch the fire bird, the tsar let his youngest son try at last.

"Ivan waited under the tree all night. Near dawn, the fire bird came and settled on the branches, inspecting the golden apples for the one that had just ripened to perfection. The fire bird was so intent on his inspection, he did not see the boy underneath the tree until it was too late. The boy grabbed the fire bird. The fire bird fought and freed itself from the boy's grasp. All that remained in the boy's hand was a feather. He watched the fire bird fly away.

"Ivan brought the feather to his father. When the tsar saw the bright colors of the feather of the fire bird, his heart was consumed with desire for the bird. Once again, the father summoned his two eldest sons. "Whichever one of you, my sons, brings me the fire bird, I will give you half of my kingdom," the tsar promised again. So, the two oldest sons set out to find the fire bird. The journey to find the fire bird was very long because the fire bird lived very far away. The way to the fire bird became so difficult that it confused and disheartened the two oldest sons of the tsar. They stopped the journey and took to amusing themselves with an easy life. Once again, the tsar was desperate. Once again, Ivan begged his father to let him find the fire bird and bring it back. Once again, the tsar reluctantly agreed and sent his youngest son to find the fire bird and bring it to his father. So, Ivan set out on his journey. Along the way, a wolf attacked Ivan and ate his horse. The boy sat down and cried. He wondered how he was going to find the fire bird without a horse to travel the great distance on. The wolf saw the boy crying and had pity. He told the boy that he would take him to the fire bird if the lad would ride on his back. So, Ivan rode the wolf to the palace of the fire bird. The palace belonged to a king who kept the fire bird in a cage. He told Ivan he would let the boy have the fire bird if the boy brought him the Horse with the Golden Mane.

"Ivan sat down to cry because he didn't know how to get the horse. The wolf pitied him again, and after the boy hopped on his back, he took him to the Horse with the Golden Mane. The Horse with the Golden Mane belonged to a king, who kept him in his palace stables. The king promised that he would give Ivan the Horse with the Golden Mane if and only if the boy would bring him a beautiful maiden named Helen. The king desired greatly to marry Helen and make her his queen.

"Before Ivan could sit down to cry again, the wolf put the boy on his back and took him to the beautiful maiden, Helen. Ivan explained to Helen that the king desired to marry her. Helen replied that she did not want to go with Ivan to marry the king because she had fallen in love with Ivan at first sight. Ivan confessed that he had also fallen in love with Helen at first sight.

"Ivan did not know what to do. The wolf took pity on him. He took the boy and Helen to the king but made them wait outside the palace in the woods. The wolf changed into a beautiful princess and promised to marry the king if he let the Horse with the Golden Mane go into the woods so that Ivan could take it to the king and exchange it for the fire bird. The king immediately agreed, but once he let the Horse with the Golden Mane go, he turned around and the princess had vanished. A wolf snarled at him, and he hid away in his palace.

"Ivan put the beautiful Helen on the Horse with the Golden Mane while he once again hopped on the wolf's back. They all rode to the palace of the fire bird. Again, the wolf tricked the king by changing into the Horse with the Golden Mane, so that the king gave Ivan the fire bird to give to his father. Again, the king found a snarling wolf instead of the Horse with the Golden Mane. The king hid in his palace.

"Ivan asked Helen to marry him, and she said yes. They promised to wed after they returned to Ivan's father, the tsar, with the fire bird *and the Horse with the Golden Mane. Ivan and Helen, with the Horse and bird, along with the wolf set out to return to the tsar. Along the way, they passed a house. Ivan's two older brothers came out of the house when they recognized Ivan. They demanded the fire bird, the Horse with Golden Mane, and the beautiful princess Helen to be given to them so that they could return to their father, the tsar, and receive half of the kingdom as a reward.*

"The wolf snarled and chased the two older brothers back into their house. The two older brothers hid in the house forever. Ivan and his companions continued on their way home. When they arrived at the palace of the tsar, they learned that the tsar had died of worry and regret over his missing sons. Ivan was crowned tsar. He married the beautiful princess Helen, and he kept the Horse with the Golden Mane in his stables and he kept the fire bird in a gilded cage in his room. Ivan thanked the wolf, and the wolf returned to his home in the forest.

"This is the story that all of the children are told in Russia. We are taught that if you try, you will succeed, especially when you find a friend who is like a wolf to help you along the way. It is like trading for furs. We will get what we came for. For our Tsarina in Russia." Demidov ended his tale with a severe stare at the Denaina men opposite of him.

There was a long awkward silence. Nicholas felt extremely uncomfortable. He liked Acts Quickly and did not see the need to provoke the Denaina chief. The chief stared calmly at Demidov with eyes that looked black in the dim lamp light. The Denaina man's face was as expressionless as a stone. Nicholas found all the faces of the Denaina guests were impassive. The tension in the air was thick.

Suddenly, Acts Quickly burst out laughing. "So much gold in your stories. Golden apples. Was the fire bird golden? Was Helen's hair golden like the horse's mane? Do Russian children like to hear about gold, gold, gold? It sounds like there are a lot of chief's or kings or tsars in Russia. Do the children want to be Tsar or Tsarina when they listen to the story? I think the wolf is the hero of the story, not Ivan." He tossed his head back and howled loudly.

The men chuckled. Demidov could not keep a giggle from escaping his lips as he was taken in by the young man's exuberance. The chief smiled as he stood up to go, and politely took his leave.

The Denaina men left quietly into the darkness beyond the fort walls. The night was still and hushed. Stars studded the sky as the Milky Way shone like a celestial river of light across the heavens. The ghost did not wail that night.

Live with wolves, howl like a wolf. Nicholas slept heavily until dawn. He rose stiffly from the work of the previous day and stretched as he stood. The cook was bustling at the stove and coffee was already brewing. The stove was warming the quarters up quickly. Nicholas grabbed a steaming cup of coffee and stepped outside. Aside from the cook, everyone else at the fort was still sleeping. The sun was just beginning to rise above the eastern horizon. Nicholas slipped out of the gate and along the trail to the bluff's edge. It was going to be a perfect day for whaling.

To Nicholas' surprise, two large skin boats were beached below the bluff. A group of eight Denaina men were busy on the shore. Nicholas descended the trail to the beach in a hurry. He found the chief, Acts Quickly, and the two cousins with four other men along the shore. They were examining something at the mouth of the small creek at the base of the bluff. As he approached, Nicholas saw that it was a wooden skiff. It was a small landing skiff from a larger sailing vessel. The skiff had a pole lying from stem to stern with a small tattered white sail attached to a cross bar. A pair of oars lay on the bottom.

The men scoured the beach for possible tracks of a wayfarer who might have disembarked from the skiff. They spread out and searched for some time before gathering back at the boat. No one could find any evidence of any persons landing and leaving the boat. They agreed it must have washed ashore on the night tide. Acts Quickly suggested that the boat was from the neighboring redoubt to the south on the Kasilof river. The incoming tide would have carried a boat from there up the shore to the Kenai River. Nicholas pulled the skiff firmly up into the creek. He explained that he was going back up to the fort to get a rope to anchor the boat more securely and tell the officers about the find. The Denaina men nodded, but insisted that they were still going to continue their hunt for beluga on the incoming tide, which was expected within the next couple of hours.

Nicholas found the officers awake and gathered around the breakfast table. They listened with interest as he relayed his adventure on the beach. Konovalov was at the table, pale and weak.

He spoke hoarsely, "It must be from Redoubt St. George at the Kasilof river. It has happened before that small boats loosened from their moorings and rode the tide to our beach. We used to have a boat with a sail in it, but it loosened from its mooring and was lost in a storm last winter. Perhaps this is the boat."

"Are you sure it isn't your ghost's boat?" Demidov asked in scorn.

Vasilev laughed as he added, "Don't look a gift horse in the mouth, right?"

Konovalov whitened. He bolted from the table to the outside. The men could hear him retching violently. After some time, there was a knock on the door. It was Igor with an arm around Konovalov, carrying him inside.

Igor looked angrily at the men. "He is not well, he should be in bed. He is vomiting blood. He has an ulcer."

Demidov shot up. "Outside, Igor, or I will have you put in chains. This is officers only quarters." He motioned to Nicholas and Vasilev to take Konovalov from Igor.

As the two men helped Konovalov up the stairs, Demidov closed the door on Igor. Konovalov moaned as he fell onto the bed. Foamy spit flecked with blood dribbled down his chin.

Vasilev pulled out a handkerchief and wiped the man's face. "No more vodka for you, Konovalov. It will kill you if you drink any more since you have an ulcer," he admonished.

He quoted the old Russian proverb, "You can't have two deaths, but you can't avoid one." They settled Konovalov under the covers and retreated downstairs.

Demidov and Vasilev stood at the table. They discussed the situation at length. It was clear that neither man appreciated Konovalov or Igor. Neither man was interested in any interaction with the Denaina whale hunt or any other activities. They both wanted to strictly carry out Zaikov's orders to please him on his return, before sailing back to civilized Russia and leaving the squalid mess at the fort.

A sturdy mooring rope was found. After the officers assigned the men their morning duties, Demidov and Vasilev followed Nicholas to the beach. They nodded to the Denaina men who were still standing by their skin boats. The Russians secured the boat to a rock up the beach above high tide. They stood a moment observing the tide begin to advance across the inlet towards the river mouth.

"This is one of the fastest and highest tides I have ever seen," commented Demidov. "I have sailed the Atlantic, the Baltic and the Black Sea. None of those areas are as harsh as this."

"What do you think of this ghost business? I have heard beluga singing. Have you? Do you think the ghost wailing is just a beluga?" Vasilev asked.

"I have heard beluga while out at sea. They didn't quite sound like the screeching the other night. I must admit that the wailing did sound like a woman. The figure looked like a woman in a white dress. It is all a mystery. This place is not for me. I don't believe in ghosts. I don't like the feel of this redoubt. Something is very wrong. Something bad. I am not superstitious or religious, but I do feel something bad here. Ominous." Demidov shook his head and turned. "There is much work to do."

Nicholas followed the men up the bluff. The three paused at the crest and looked back. The tide was now beating back the river currents in huge waves as the salt water pushed up the river. The Denaina boats had launched. The Russians saw the white backs of a pod of beluga whales as they entered the river and swam upstream. The Denaina men paddled hard to follow the whales.

"The boats are so light. The construction of wood frame and skin makes the boats fast and easy to paddle upstream," Vasilev admired. They enjoyed the chase until the whales and men rounded a river bend upstream beyond sight.

"Have you ever eaten beluga?" Vasilev asked his companions. Nicholas shook his head as Vasilev continued. "As a matter of fact, I have. We killed some when we sailed in the Bering Sea. We were quite hungry for fresh food and the stores were low. It was quite tasty. A little fishy and a little chewy, but quite tasty." Demidov smiled.

The day was hot. The men at the redoubt sweated as they worked hard throughout the sweltering hours. Cutting the rough timbers into useful boards proved to be more difficult because of knotty logs. When the sun sank low over the mountains to the west, Demidov called an early end to the labor. The men dashed to the creek and bathed. The Denaina people were nowhere in sight. Clean and refreshed, the men lounged around the fort until dinner time. They ate heartily and sat the rest of the evening watching the sun set and the stars which started to appear in the clear sky. The night was beginning to settle when Spear and Acts Quickly arrived at the gate. They brought several baskets of beluga meat. Acts Quickly explained that the villagers had harvested two belugas after a long hunt and spent the rest of the day dressing the whales.

He invited the men to the feast at the village, which was now beginning and would go late into the night. Demidov declined, but accepted the meat and thanked Acts Quickly. The young Denaina men disappeared into the darkness.

The redoubt settled into quiet. Men sought their beds, stretching their weary limbs and quickly falling asleep. Nicholas found his spare bed under the stairs and groaned softly as he laid his length out. It felt good to be clean again after perspiring work all day in the hot sun. He momentarily regretted missing the excitement of the whale hunt and fell into a deep sleep.

Two hours later, pandemonium erupted at the fort. The furious barking of the dogs snapped Nicholas awake. In alarm, he began dressing. Footsteps thudded down the stairs as Demidov and Vasilev raced to the door with their clothes hastily donned and pistols drawn.

"What is going on?" yelled Demidov as he dashed out the door with Vasilev on his heels. Nicholas lit a lantern and stepped out.

Behind him, Konovalov peered over his shoulder, whispering, "What is it?"

The dogs stood snarling at the front gate. Men poured out of the barracks. The two watchmen were standing by the fire and pointing.

One of the watchmen screamed, "Medved. Medved."

Rifles were brought and men fired at the gate. Slats were broken and a large gap was opened. There, a monstrous brown bear reared and roared. A mighty paw smashed the boards, and the entire front wall of the fort shook. The watchmen bravely grabbed wood from the fires' edge while dashing towards the bear and thrust the burning logs towards the bruin. The bear growled as it dropped down and disappeared into the blackness beyond. Shaken, the men hurried to cover the gap with whatever wood they could find around the fort.

"I don't think the bear will return tonight. It must have smelled the fresh beluga meat," Demidov spoke as he tested the makeshift wall over the gap. "Between the dogs and the fire, I am sure the bear is frightened off for good. Tomorrow, in daylight, we will look for it around the fort and kill it if we find it. Good night, men."

The officers watched as the men returned to their barracks, and made sure the watchmen were at the fire before they returned to their beds. Konovalov was silent as he returned to his rest. Demidov and Vasilev ignored him. Nicholas closed his eyes wearily the moment before he fell prone. The break in sleep had made him even more tired.

Nicholas had not yet begun dreaming in deep sleep when he was again startled awake by loud screaming. He sat up, trying to figure out what was going on. Konovalov was screaming upstairs. Dogs were howling outside. The night had changed. Wind was whistling in the cracks of the building. In the distance, under the din of the dogs, the wind and Konovalov, Nicholas thought he heard a woman scream. He started. Upstairs, Demidov, whose patience had run out, was cursing and yelling at Konovalov to shut up. Nicholas heard Vasilev rise and cross the room to Konovalov's bed where there was the sound of a loud slap. Konovalov began whimpering. Outside, men were yelling at the dogs to stop howling. Some other men began to wail in fear. Nicholas lit another lantern as Demidov thundered down the stairs. He yanked open the door and roared at the men. The dogs whined and quieted at the officer's voice. The men were stunned into silence.

"Shut up. Shut up and go back to bed. Go on, you fools." Demidov glared at the men as Nicholas joined him on the porch, holding the lantern high.

The men sullenly slipped off one by one to their quarters. Demidov turned to Nicholas, opened his mouth, and clamped it tightly shut before stamping furiously back upstairs. Nicholas extinguished the lamp and lay down again. He stared into the blackness of the room, unable to quit listening. Faintly, above the wind, a woman wailed in the darkness from beyond the bluff. He did not know if any of the others heard it too. Konovalov had stopped whimpering and the upstairs was silent. Nicholas lay awake for several hours before his fatigue overcame him, and he dozed off uneasily.

EIGHT

BANG. NICHOLAS' EYES FLEW OPEN. Cook began cursing as he slammed a pot on the wood stove. Smoke was filling the room. Nicholas pulled his boots on and fled outside, coughing from the smoke. The clouds had moved in overnight and now hung low. The yard was dark. The fort was full of shadows. One lonely, ragged watchman sat by the last embers of the fire, his chin on his chest. A rusted rifle leaned against his leg. No one else was in sight. The cook appeared at the door behind Nicholas, flapping his apron as smoke billowed out of the quarters. He grimaced at Nicholas. There was coughing upstairs and the thud of boots down the steps as the officers filed down, disheveled and dreary. Konovalov was missing.

Demidov summarized the day's orders over breakfast as Vasilev agreed. The officers would carry rifles and pistols to guard the men as they worked to fix the gap in the fort. They discussed Konovalov. Demidov warned that he would have the man chained in one of the sheds and returned to Russia to be put in an asylum for the insane. Vasilev countered that if the fort commander stayed to his bed until Zaikov returned, they would let the Captain handle the situation. He insisted that they inventory all the firearms and weapons for defense and organize a plan of protection against any threat. Nicholas and Demidov agreed.

Demidov shook his head in disgust as he reviewed the pile of rifles on the porch. Vasilev sighed as he counted the musket balls and pouches of gunpowder. Nicholas surveyed the weapons as a cold chill ran up his spine. He felt infinitely far from home, naked and exposed in the brutal wilderness. He glanced at his fellow officers, whose faces were grim with the same realization of vulnerability.

"The redoubt is a shameful mess," Demidov growled.

Vasilev clapped the officer's back and said lightheartedly, "We will have to make do with what we have. We are not at war. The natives are friendly and give us beluga. Zaikov is returning in just over a week. So let us do what we can and be ready when it is time to go. Let us make the best of the situation." He smiled encouragingly at his companions.

Nicholas and Demidov shrugged off the ominous feeling and smiled back at Vasilev. "Your cheer is too much to resist," Demidov murmured.

The officers fell into discussion. They tried to decide which was the more important task for the men that day. Should the work on the fort be paused while the men cleaned rifles and practiced some defense tactics, or should the fort be repaired and then the rifles readied for any sort of attack? Vasilev insisted that the current weather was a window of opportunity for fixing the fort, while the rifles could be cleaned if the weather turned bad. He reminded the officers that there seemed to be no real threat to the fort that called for firearms if the walls shut out all dangers. Demidov reluctantly agreed. The men organized themselves and chose several capable men carry rifles and oversee the crews as they rebuilt the fort walls. Once the decision was made, the sky seemed to clear, and the wind died to a tiny whisper. The men ate and set to work with a resolution, singing and laughing heartily. The dogs were let out of the fort and allowed to follow the men as they hauled the timbers from the piles in the woods behind. There was no sign of any bears, and anxieties dissipated as the sun streamed brightly on the fort.

By noon, a breeze began to rise from the north. An hour later, a thick fog bank swept down the inlet. As late afternoon turned to evening, the fog engulfed the fort. Shirts and coats that had been pulled off while working were now hastily donned as men shivered with the deepening chill. It was gloomy, dull and dank. When the men stopped working, all sounds were eerily hushed by the fog. It looked like a dark cold night lay ahead. Vasilev called off the workday for lack of light to see by and the men quickly turned to their quarters to start fires for cooking, light and warming their shelter.

Nicholas shivered. He looked around for his overcoat and remembered he had cast it off near the log pile outside the fort.

"Coming in for tea?" called Vasilev from the door of the officer's quarters. Nicholas nodded and explained he was getting his coat from the log pile.

"On your way in, see to it that the door to the fort is shut tight," said Vasilev.

Nicholas strode across the compound. The fog had become so thick that an icy film was sticking to every exposed surface, and a man could barely make out the walls of the fort several yards ahead of him. He passed one of the men who was leading the dogs inside for the night as they growled and whimpered.

He kept an arm's length from the outer fort wall as he made his way carefully to the logs. His teeth were chattering as he groped for his coat, found it, and pulled it tightly on. He turned back the way he had come. Then a hand was over his mouth and an iron grasp pinned his arms. He was immediately immobilized by an unseen assailant from behind him. His heart pounded in shock and adrenaline flushed his veins. He couldn't reach his pistol or his knife. He weighed how to struggle against the hold.

Urgent words were whispered in his ear, "I am not going to hurt you. Be quiet and I will let you go. I want to show you something. Come with me." Acts Quickly!

Nicholas' mind raced. What was Acts Quickly going to do?

"I have to tell you something. You must come see the ghost tonight. I think you will find what you came here for," Acts Quickly continued whispering.

Nicholas didn't move or speak, he let his body relax so the Acts Quickly could feel he did not intend to sound an alarm or fight.

Acts Quickly insisted as he let Nicholas loose, "Come with me. Don't yell or try to run. I want you to come with me. I think I understand now why you came here from Russia."

Nicholas remained still, his body ready to spring in defensive combat as the Acts Quickly went on, "I have two men with me, Nicholas. We come in peace. I want to show you something and you will understand. Everything will be clear."

Two sturdy Denaina men stepped from around the log pile out of the gloom. They were shorter than the chief's son, but as muscular in build and fiercely intense. They held hunting muskets in their hands and knives on their belts. Nicholas looked into their dark eyes and knew they were warriors. He stayed still. Acts Quickly motioned to them to relax. They stopped and stood ready for a fight, their face betraying their mistrust of Nicholas.

"You are lucky I didn't shoot you. There was a bear here last night. It broke into the fort wall," Nicholas said to the natives. He was not prepared for the laughter that met his words.

"Ggagga wanted beluga," Acts Quickly chuckled. "The brown bear came to our village after you Russians scared him off. Spear killed him. It took us all night to skin and burn the bear. Spear will take the bear hide to the fort tomorrow and show the men how big the bruin was. Spear is a fearless hunter." There was more laughter.

"Let me go back, eat supper and wait for the other officers to retire for the night. I will get a lantern," Nicholas said.

He quickly added as the Denaina shifted uneasily, "They will come looking for me. Then, you will have a fight. They all have guns. Let me do this and there will be no trouble."

Acts Quickly considered his words a moment. Then, he nodded. He gave a low whistle and told Nicholas to come to the fort door and whistle when he was ready to go with them. The men followed Nicholas to the entrance.

"I'll be back," Nicholas reassured Acts Quickly. He looked back, but the Denaina men had disappeared into the gloom. He entered the fort.

The courtyard was quiet. The rest of yesterday's stew had been quickly reheated and eaten heartily before the weary men who had worked hard all day at fixing up the fort now fell into their beds. The officers' quarters were warm, and the men ate quietly at the table. All memories of the disturbances of the night before were banished from thought. Nicholas' companions spoke of how good it felt to work hard in the fresh air on land after months aboard the St. George sailing from Russia. They agreed that the work was also tiring. Demidov and Vasilev immediately ascended the stairs after finishing their meal, yawning widely.

Shortly afterwards, Nicholas heard heavy snores from the loft. He grabbed a lantern and coat and slipped outside. The fog was denser now and the light of the fires in the fort weakly penetrated the thick gloom. He could barely see across the yard. He tiptoed to the fort door and eased through, careful to close it firmly behind him. He gave a low whistle muffled by the heavy fog. Instantly, the Denaina men were beside him.

"Follow us," Acts Quickly said quietly.

Nicholas followed him as the two men flanked him. Acts Quickly lithely strode from the entrance to the fort and away from the bluff trail into the woods, where a wide path opened. It curved behind the fort towards the Denaina village on the river. Nicholas hurried to keep Acts Quickly in sight amidst the darkening fog. The sounds of the fort died away, stifled by the heavy, damp air and rising gales. Adrenaline and excitement filled Nicholas. Contrary to the circumstances, he felt unafraid, and all his senses were heightened. Every minute detail and sound were clear. His feet were sure as he loped after Acts Quickly. He understood without a doubt that the Denaina did not wish him any harm. Acts Quickly had talked about the ghost. Perhaps he would solve the mystery and find out what evil Konovalov and Balushin were hiding. He wanted to put the fear of Rusalka to rest by the time Zaikov returned.

The Denaina village was near the river. Nicholas recalled how Konovalov had explained earlier that the first Russians who arrived at the river had referred to the natives as Kenaitze, or people of the flats, when they reported back to the redoubt near the Kasilof river. The brume was denser at this lower level. The village was quiescent and obscure, save two fires barely distinguishable in the haze. Illusions of spare log structures alluded to homes in the shady billows of mist. Several dogs barked and then fell silent as the men called softly in their language. In the foggy shadows, Nicholas couldn't clearly make out the dwellings and Acts Quickly led him through the village to the bank of the river. Nicholas could hear the currents gurgling past in the blackness.

A group of men gathered on the gravel around a tiny fire. A tall older man stepped forward. He spoke to Acts Quickly as Nicholas stood eyeing the Denaina men who now encircled him. Acts Quickly joined Nicholas, handing him back his pistol.

"Remember, this is my father. He is our chief. He doesn't like to speak in Russian in our village. He knows why you are here. He wants to help you."

Nicholas nodded at the man, studying him carefully. He wondered how the chief could possibly know the reason for his journey to the fort and immediately dismissed any answer that came to mind. Whatever the natives were intending, he would see, but as far as he knew no one knew why he had come to the Kenay Redoubt.

The chief spoke to his son in Denaina.

Acts Quickly nodded and turned to the Russian. "I am going to take you across the river. You will see for yourself whether the ghost is real or not. I will tell you everything. The Russians did something bad and that is why they think there is a ghost. They are afraid because they are guilty. But I will take you to the ghost. You will see and understand. You must come with me now."

The chief nodded silently as his son spoke. He gestured across the river.

Nicholas was silent, studying the men around him. They all nodded at him and pointed across the river. He could see no threat in their eyes. A man picked up the lantern from beside the fire and lit the candle before giving it to Acts Quickly. He lifted the lantern and led the way down to a canoe beached on the edge of the bank. The craft was barely big enough for two men with a skin covering the hull. The men handed Acts Quickly some articles of clothing. He donned a light jacket, pants and a pair of boots. There was a second set for Nicholas. The clothes were made of a light material. Nicholas slipped the light boots over his own. Acts Quickly explained that the clothes were made of animal guts which had been dried and sewn as waterproof apparel for the trip. The chief handed his son a leather bag and a pistol. Acts Quickly packed the bag in the stern and belted the pistol on securely. He settled Nicholas in the boat holding the lantern aloft.

He pushed the craft off the sandbar and jumped lightly in with a neatly carved wooden paddle in his hand. "We will ride the tide. It is coming in now."

The mighty Kenai River currents had hushed. The incoming tide flowed in, filling the river mouth. Nicholas watched the bank and the tiny fire on the beach disappear instantly in the fog. A gust of wind slammed the starboard side of the frail barque. Acts Quickly immediately paddled the stern to the wind. A stronger gust followed and pushed the craft up the river on the tide. Acts Quickly worked the vessel carefully across the river so that Nicholas' lantern lit the edge of the sand on the far side through the blowing mists. He thought the Acts Quickly would bank the boat so they could explore the far shore where the Russians had heard the ghost scream and seen it hover over the sands. But to his surprise, they followed the bank upriver. Nicholas braced his arm on the side of the boat to keep the wind from knocking the lantern from his hand into the water. He could not recall a time he felt more alive or thrilled. The wind threatened to sweep any words he would speak away into the night, so he held his silence even as his mind raced with questions for Acts Quickly.

Acts Quickly peered at the shoreline through the clouds of dense fog that raced along on the gusts and fought the force of the wind and tide to keep the boat from turning broadside and capsizing. The gusts were intensifying now. A sharp chop of white capped waves lapped in the dim lantern glow. The increasing roar of the air and water was terrifying. Fog blew by in sheets, revealing glimpses here and there of where they were going. The craft began to buck unsteadily. Just when Nicholas was about to yell that it was too dangerous to go on, Acts Quickly paddled with mighty strokes towards the sandy shore. Nicholas gripped the side of the boat, unable to speak, and sure that the boat would capsize as the starboard was broad to the gust. He readied himself to swim to shore, certain that he would be plunged into the icy waves at any second. Acts Quickly thrust the paddle swiftly and ducked. The gust of wind and fog screamed over them and then the water calmed. Nicholas held up the lantern. They were in a narrow side channel below the sandbar which blocked the wind.

Acts Quickly grinned sheepishly. He said something in his language and then remembered to speak Russian. He chuckled. "That was exciting."

Nicholas shook his head. "Where are we?" he asked.

Acts Quickly explained that the river delta had many small waterways that filled up on the high tide, making it easy to cross the flat to the other side. As he spoke, the boat floated steadily up the channel on the incoming tide. Grasses whistled in the gusts along the bank above them on either side as if the wind was angrily looking for them. Below the line of grasses, the channel consisted of slimy banks of quicksand that would be impossible to walk on.

Acts Quickly gently guided the boat through the channel, letting the tide carry them forward. The channel doubled back and curved on itself. He kept a careful watch on the waterway, holding the paddle ready, and talking about the tides. Some of the tides were so high in the fall that the entire river delta was covered with water. The tide also advanced several miles up the river, flooding the trees on the river bottom. One of the highest tides was on this night. The wind usually blew on the leading edge of the tide. But tonight, a storm had blown in and the winds pushed the tide in early and higher. He talked on as they patiently rode the flooding current across the flats. Nicholas listened in fascination.

After a time, the beach grass gave way to small willows and an occasional spruce or birch tree. Then, the channel rounded a final corner and a cut bank lined with trees rose over them. Acts Quickly followed the waterway further to a dip in the bank where a small rocky cove lay. He paddled the bow onto the tiny beach.

Nicholas jumped ashore and pulled the nose of the bow up onto the bank. Acts Quickly leapt easily from the boat, and together they pulled the boat safely from the water's edge. Nicholas stood up and held the lantern up to light the trail up the bank.

His breath was caught in his throat as he froze in total shock.

Above him on the bank stood the ghost. A walking corpse of white clothed in a filmy white dress with tatters that waved on the wind. The specter opened its mouth as if to begin screaming.

NINE

*P*RIZRAK. *GHOST.* NO SOUND UTTERED FROM the mouth of the white wraith. A blast of wind roared down the bank, shaking trees and whistling in the men's ears. Nicholas crossed himself hastily, momentarily shaken with doubt. *There before him stood Rusalka.*

"*Nicholas.*" The wraith called his name under the winds, screeching forth. Chills ran up Nicholas' spine. He didn't believe in ghosts. He darted a look at Acts Quickly. Acts Quickly was not afraid. He gathered a small leather bag he had carried from the village and started up the bank. He gestured for Nicholas to follow. Nicholas' heart was pounding in his chest as he scrambled up the bank. Acts Quickly stood beside the specter and turned to Nicholas. "Sophia."

Nicholas studied the ghost face to face. It was a woman.

She was so tall her eyes were almost level with Nicholas. She was scrutinizing him in return. She was gravely emaciated. Her eyes were sunken and darkened underneath, but the color in her right eye was a deep violet while the left eye was a brilliant green that shone in the pale lantern rays. Her skin was stretched over the bones of her face, which were gaunt and hollow. Her arms showed through the tatters of what remained of a white wedding dress, bony and long. A worn and stained short coat of white arctic fox fur fitted over the dress. Her feet were covered with native boots just like the ones Nicholas had donned over his. Long ragged strands of golden hair blew about her shoulders and face. There was something about her bearing that intrigued Nicholas instantly.

"There will no going back until the next tide." Acts Quickly's words broke their mutual inspection. "Sophia?" She stepped forward. The fog was clearing on this side of the river. They began to follow the trail.

A wall of alder lined the bank and formed a tangled fence. Behind the alder grew thick willow brushes whose tops whipped several feet above their heads in the gale. The narrow trail mounted the uppermost bluff above the floodplain of the river. The willows gave way to birches. The path rose at a steady incline across the face of the ridge from east to west. There was no fog, and the wind was now tamed in the tops of towering white spruce stands. The air was warmer at the crest. The path led along the top of the bluff, just inside the spruce trees so that one could traverse the edge while viewing the inlet, the entire river flat, the fort, or the Denaina village to the mountain ranges beyond. Yet, the hiker would not be easily seen by anyone looking at the ridge because of the dense screen of tree cover.

Nicholas saw stars above and their reflection on the snow of Mount Redoubt. The air was now a soft sighing in the boughs high over his head. His nostrils were filled by the pungent dankness of moss and mushroom growing from the spongy ground.

The trail left the overlook and cut due south. The ridge gave way to a cut, and in the middle was a knoll. There, nestled amid the forest, stood a humble log cabin at the knoll's sheltered crest. It was shielded snugly out of sight from the views of the inlet. Nicholas could smell the scent of wood smoke from a stove from within the cabin.

Despite its quaint surroundings, the cabin was an abode of refined and skilled woodwork, the best Nicholas had seen since his arrival in Kenay. He recognized the familiar square logs as Russian handicraft. It had a miniature covered porch that overlooked the cut where he could hear the water of a small spring gurgling below. The walls and doors were solid. There were no windows, but a tiny turret rose out of the roof so that a person could stand in the turret and look in all directions, like a small castle in the midst of a harsh wilderness.

Sophia led the way into the cabin and took the lantern from Nicholas to set on the table in the center of the room. Nicholas looked around. The interior of the cabin matched the craftsmanship of the exterior. There was a stove, table, several chairs, a counter and wash basin, shelves, and a bed along the far side. It was warm and invitingly cozy, giving one a feeling of safety from the cold and dark wildness outside.

Acts Quickly placed the leather sack on the table.

Sophia eagerly opened it and pulled out the contents. "Candles. I was out and had to sit in the dark or open the stove for light."

She tore off a piece of a loaf of bread and ate it in quick hungry bites. There was sugar, tea, and meat. Nicholas looked at Acts Quickly in wonder as she pulled out potatoes and a cabbage.

Acts Quickly laughed. "The new priest brought these things to my father yesterday. He was looking for word of Father Juvenal and where he could find him."

The three drank cups of tea with slices of bread while a pot of stew boiled vigorously on the stove. When the stew was done, they ate. There was little talk. and Nicholas realized the night would soon turn to dawn.

At last, Sophia addressed Nicholas. "Thank you for coming.

Acts Quickly said he would bring you." Nicholas nodded.

Sophia's hand pushed her hair back and she straightened herself elegantly. "I am Sophia Elizabeth Anna Fyodorovich, daughter of Pyotr Fyodorovich, Emperor of Russia."

The air in the cabin was still in the following hush. Nicholas stared at her directly and she met his gaze evenly. He could see her royal lineage and grace had not faded with starvation.

Acts Quickly broke the silence. "She is the true Tsarina of your Russia. You came to get her."

Thoughts swirled in Nicholas' mind, and it all began to make sense to him why fate had brought him here to the tiny cabin in the woods. He thought of the wealthy banker from St. Petersburg who paid exorbitantly for his rank and passage on the ship. He recalled the enigmatic directive to 'find a young woman of good Russian blood who was taken to Alaska and bring her back.' The banker, Viktor Perov, had complained that the Tsarina Catherine the Great was an obstacle to the bank's interest in Alaska because she ignored the Lebedev Company in favor of interests elsewhere in the world, such as in China. Catherine was getting old and had lost her way by reading Voltaire and adopting new notions of how society should be formed.

The young woman, Sophia, was intended to be brought back from Kenai and presented to Catherine to set the Tsarina's views on Alaska aright. She would give a first-hand account of the importance of the Lebedev Company's success and profitability in Alaska. She would use feminine diplomacy with Catherine, and the sole developmental control of Alaska's riches of furs, lands, and resources would be given to the Lebedev Company, the bank and its inner group of wealthy traders. Nicholas would receive a title of nobility, land, and equally exorbitant payment for the successful return of Sophia. Then, there had followed a lengthy discourse on the urgency of political matters and the security of the entire

Russian Empire. But the banker had never mentioned that the young woman was the rightful Tsarina.

As Nicholas leaned forward to ask a question, Sophia held up her hand. "I will tell you everything. Then you will understand."

"My story begins in Ropsha. See here," she produced a leather-bound manuscript. It was divided into two sections. The first was written firmly by a man's hand, and the second in a graceful, feminine hand. "Read it. You will understand." Nicholas began.

Karl Peter Ulrich is my name. I am the rightful Emperor of Russia. I write this in haste as I have been arrested and fear for my unjust murder by the order of Sophie Frederica Auguste, princess of Anhalt Zerbst, now converted to Ekaterina Alexeievna, or Catherine. I was born in Kiel because my father was the Duke of Holstein Gottorp. My grandfathers were Peter the Great of Russia and Charles XII of Sweden. My parents died when I was only 14 and my aunt Elizabeth was Empress of Russia. It was she who arranged my young marriage to Catherine with the best of my interests at heart. We had to be converted to Russian Orthodoxy to please our Russian subjects. I was renamed Pyotr Fyodorovich or Peter the Third. Catherine was ruthless from the moment the arrangement was made known to her. Her face was filled with lust for power and hatred for me. I cannot say she turned against me, as she was never for me. Our marriage was never consummated. I could not bear to go near this woman who openly despised me for my birthright and my title. Catherine used every whim and trick to have me arrested and imprisoned in Ropsha. For a time, no one knew where I was hidden, as I had been exiled by Catharine. Elizabeth, my aunt, searched diligently for me. After finding me, Elizabeth arranged for the monks of the nearby monastery to visit me. Through the priests, I got word to Elizabeth that my marriage had never been consummated and Catherine had mocked me by having affairs openly. With the help of the Patriarch, it was decided that I should have an annulment of the marriage and marry another princess, Joanna, from Sweden. Then, Elizabeth would gather the help of loyal members of the royal court and the monastery to throw Catherine in prison and crown me as Tsar of Russia, but I prayed to God to send me back to Holstein and Prussia. I hate this horrible cold place. I hate the uncivilized horror of Ropsha, Russia! My Aunt Elizabeth is my only hope for freedom.

A year and a half have passed since I began this record. Joanna and I have found that bliss that no man has a right to in this Godforsaken land of bitter cold. Our daughter is but six months old. She has inherited the singular trait of Joanna and all her royal ancestors. Her right eye is deep violet, and her left eye is green. She has also inherited my trait of having the little finger on the left hand bending inward. One only has to look at her to know she is the child of Peter, Tsar of Russia and Joanna of the house of the King of Sweden. Her beauty is no less than Joanna's. I have named her Sophia Elizabeth Anna. She is a child of grace and deeply intelligent. Here, in this tiny miserable house, I have experienced the joy of family that was stolen from me by my parents' death and the cruelty of my tutors. Joanna is a saintly woman, she never complains and does the work of a servant, which she is not accustomed to. The cold cracks her hands and yet she waits patiently for that day when I will be Tsar.

The priest came today. He brought a note from Elizabeth. Catherine has bought spies at an exorbitant price here in Ropsha. She knows that I have told Elizabeth that the marriage was never consummated. She is terrified she will lose her power. Catherine has sent men to kill me.

I have little time left. I write this for you, my precious daughter, my Sophia. I have made an arrangement with the monks to take your mother and you into hiding. With my seal and signet ring, you will one day rule Russia. You are the rightful Tsarina, my love. I pray you will become the beautiful, blessed, Tsarina Sophia and banish all the evil that the first Sophie, now Catherine, has done. I love you always.

The firm handwriting ended. The page was wrinkled and tattered. There was a dull brown spot on one corner. Nicholas wondered if it was the Tsar's blood. He looked up at Sophia.

"Read on," she commanded, as she rose to add wood to the stove. Nicholas bent over the next page. It had marks on the side. He knew at once they were made by tears.

I am of age today. That's what the nuns say. What does it mean? Oh, Papa, how I wish you were here. Oh, Momma, how I wish you were here. I am alone. I am so alone. Now that I am of age, Father Juvenal has sat me down and given me this ledger of Papa's, to tell me the story of my past and write my own future records in. He showed me how my little finger on my left-hand bent inward, a trait inherited from my father. He assured me that the heterochromia of the kind that I have in my eyes, one violet and one green, was so rare that one only had to look at me to know I was the daughter of Joanna. I now understand why I was always kept apart. I now understand why the other girls at the monastery school were not allowed to socialize with me. I had no one. As sure as the eyes in my head and the finger of my hand, I am the true Tsarina of Russia.

My only memory of Papa and Mama was the last time I remember being warm. Until Father Juvenal described my parents and our home in Ropsha, I wasn't sure if the memory was a real one of my own parents or a dream of what I wanted my parents to be. My memory is of a warm room in a bright house (the monastery was never bright, and always bleak) where a tall man stood in front of the fireplace. He was tall, blond with brilliant blue eyes and a handsome uniform. A woman sat on a sofa. She had long golden hair that shone in the light. She was so beautiful. Her eyes were different colors, twinkling in the lights, and she was tall and elegant in a white dress with a fur throw over her shoulders. I was sitting on the rug at her feet. The man swooped me up in his arms and the woman laughed. Her laughter sounded so sweet, and I knew the man loved her and me. He kissed my cheek just as the door opened. Soldiers came in and the man and woman were alarmed. I was taken to a room for a nap, and I do not remember anything else about that beautiful warm home.

Father Juvenal showed me a signet ring used for setting wax seals. It was my father's. He said a man was coming to meet me that afternoon and a plan would be laid out for my future. The man arrived later. He was very wealthy. He said he was a banker from St. Petersburg. He and Father Juvenal talked a long time and studied maps on the table. Then, the man bowed to me and smiled. His eyes glinted and he held his finger to his lips.

"Take care of our Tsarina, Father. Don't let Catherine find out about her. The future belongs to our dear Sophia. When the time is right, she will be crowned Empress of Russia." He left immediately.

I had no time to ask questions. Father Juvenal called the Mother Superior of the monastery. Before I knew it, another nun, Sister Xenia, and I were seated on the train beside Father Juvenal. I was dressed as a nun, a nun with a vow of silence. We were also trained as nurses at the monastery, which was the reason we accompanied the priest, so we could minister the bodies of the sick while he ministered to the soul. He explained to the conductor that he was traveling to the Far East and on to Alaska to establish a mission among the native people at the fur trading fort. Thus, my journey across Russia and deeper into the cold country began, despite my aversion to the cold climate and deep longing for warm sunny lands. Sister Xenia was only a year older than me. She had just taken her permanent vows. She was quiet, reserved, patient and kind. She took care of me like a lady's maid. It was a grueling journey of long suffering. I was hungry, tired, uncomfortable, and always cold, cold, cold. We traveled by train, horse cart, walking and sailing, until we finally reached Petropavlovsk in Kamchatka. There was a tiny monastery there and since Sister Xenia had become ill, we left her there to board our vessel to Alaska. I cried to leave the beloved nun, who was the only companion and friend I had ever known to show me tenderness and loyalty in all my life.

The long difficult journey gave Father Juvenal the time to tell me everything. He gave me an account of my parents' last moments and how I came to be an orphan in the monastery near Ropsha, hidden from the world. In the final days, friends of my father and his aunt, Elizabeth, were warned of Catherine's spies, who were scouring the country in search of us. Catherine had become paranoid that my father would return to St. Petersburg, reveal that the marriage was never consummated, and throw her from the throne. The spies had learned that there was a beautiful woman of royal lineage who had been smuggled from Europe to Ropsha, and that she was living with my father in his exile. Catherine sent men to assassinate my parents. My father had become deeply devout in his religion and was very close to the monks and nuns of the monastery near Ropsha. He paid them a great sum of gold through Elizabeth to hide and educate me at the monastery if something should happen to him. When I turned sixteen, I was to be smuggled out of Russia to Sweden. I was to present the signet ring and physical attributes proving my true identity to my mother's relatives. There, I would be educated at court and gather support from the kings of Europe to expose Catherine as a usurper and overthrow her rule, taking the Russian throne as my own.

Father Juvenal had arranged for me to go with him, disguised as a missionary religious nurse, to Alaska. The banker was supposed to contact trusted allies in Europe. A ship would be sent for me from England or even Spain. If no ship came, Father Juvenal intended to take me with him to California and arrange for me to travel across the United States to New York, where friends of my father lived. I would sail to Sweden from New York. In my meager luggage, I had this leather-bound record of my father's, a single white dress to change out of my religious habit, the signet ring, and a fur wrap. I longed to take off the heavy nun's habit and put on the beautiful white dress and fur wrap and dance around freely. Instead, I had to wear a veil and hide my face, for fear of anyone seeing my eyes. So, when we set sail on Saint George the Victorious, Father Juvenal was very concerned with my being the only woman on the vessel. Although Captain Zaikov was an honorable man who demanded the respect of his crew, he and Father Juvenal agreed to keep me locked in my tiny quarters during the time at sea. Since I was seasick most of the time, I was relieved to stay in. Towards the end of the journey, I longed to go on deck and breathe the cold clear air of Alaska.

When we finally arrived at the Redoubt Kenay, Gregori Konovalov and Amos Balushin were in command. Captain Zaikov was angry about the condition of the fort and demanded that the men build Father Juvenal a proper church and mission quarters. He was only dropping us off and would return in a year or so. I wonder when the Captain returns if the conditions of the fort will be worse!

At once, Father Juvenal set about establishing his mission. Since the Russian men at the fort were wild and prone to drinking and carousing, he turned to the Denaina natives to evangelize the Gospel. Good Father Juvenal was a holy man, and the native people quickly grew to love him. We were invited to stay in the village in two tiny, one-room cabins that sat side by side, sharing a wall. The chief's son, Acts Quickly, learned Russian quickly and through his interpreting, Father Juvenal was able to gain many believers. My nursing skills were put to use amongst the villagers. We enjoyed a time of peace and growing charity as the mission grew. The chief told neighboring native people about the 'good Russian priest and his kind healing nun.' Father Juvenal built the log cabin across the river on the south bank, hidden in the trees, unknown to the

Russians at the fort. The cabin was sturdy and isolated. Father often retreated there to pray in peace and quiet. He dreamed of building a school and monastery there. But, fate took an ugly turn and the forces of darkness opposed the light of Father Juvenal.

The Denaina women are very becoming and of these beautiful women, one stood out in exceptional grace and elegance. She was the chief's daughter and older sister of Acts Quickly. Her Denaina name was Tsik'esdlagh, for her voice was like an angel and she sang like a songbird, the sparrow. She was loved by all, and we all simply called her Ada which, in her Denaina tongue, means 'dear one'. She was very shy and reserved and did not want to attract attention. When Father Juvenal told her about the Christ and taught her about the faith, she was devout and eager to serve her "Naq'eltani" or "beloved supreme Chief." As soon as Father taught her about the faith, she begged to be baptized and took the name of Anna. Anna was as intelligent as she was beautiful, learning Russian easily and reading and writing whenever Father or I could give her lessons.

Thus, during the first seasons of our time among the Denaina, we were joyful. We shared their lives and learned their ways as they welcomed us. There was an abundance of all thing: rich food, warm fur clothes, singing and dancing, wandering the land and exploring the waters. Father Juvenal left me at times to visit nearby villages to bring them the sacraments. Anna stayed with me, and her family watched over us. Acts Quickly was a highly skilled hunter and trapper. He took us in his watercraft made of skin and wood. We went up the river and on calm days, we went along the shore of the inlet. We watched eagles, caribou, moose, bears and wolves. We picked berries and gathered roots and plants. When the first winter came, we wore snowshoes and rode in the dog sleds. Winter passed shortly and spring began.

Anna was earnest in her religious practice. She desired to

become a nun and give her life entirely to the Lord. Father Juvenal was pleased and contemplated how to fulfill her vocation. He talked about sending for more missionary priests and nuns. He went to the fort with a letter to be sent to his mission which he entrusted to Konovalov. When Father Juvenal returned, I could see that something was bothering him. I asked him what the matter was. He answered that he wanted me to stay indoors. When he had given the letter to Konovalov, he and Balushin began asking questions about what Father was doing among the Denaina. They were looking for a way to get more furs from the villagers. Father was worried they would come to the village and make trouble. That night, there was a loud knock on the door. Acts Quickly was there. An elderly Denaina woman was dying in the nearby village and had asked for the priest. Father Juvenal dressed hastily and departed, leaving Anna and me alone.

The next morning was warm and bright. Anna and I went to the river and washed our clothes. Afterwards, Anna wanted to walk down the riverbank to the beach below the bluff where the fort stood in the sun while the tide was low. Cottonwood grew at the bottom of the bluff, and she wanted to look for the fragrant waxy buds to pick for making medicinal salves. We started out only to find that a section of the bank was impassable because the river channel had washed away any sandbar for walking on. Anna decided to get the skin boat and drift down to the sandy beach, where we landed easily because the tide was out. We were soon busy searching the cotton woods when we were startled by a man's voice.

"Aren't you pretty." It was Konovalov on the bluff above us. "Look here, Amos. A pair of pretty birds."

Balushin was straining to see through the trees. "Women. It's been so long since I have seen a woman in this godforsaken place." To our horror, there was the sound of feet scrambling down the bluff trail.

"Run," Anna whispered. She yanked my hand and dragged me towards the boat. We ran from the trees and dashed across the sand. We jumped in the light boat and Anna pushed us from shore into the water with the paddle. The men had reached the far end of the beach and were racing towards us. They looked like beasts ready to attack helpless prey. Their dark hairy faces were contorted.

When the tide is low, the raging current of the Kenai River is laid bare. It sweeps down into the inlet waters where the tops of boulders loom up from the silty mud. Immediately, we knew we were in trouble. Anna paddled bravely and the light skin boat skimmed across the top of the current. She steered the bow up the river at a diagonal to cross, for we both knew that it was impossible to return the way we had drifted down from the village and safety. The men stood at the edge of the water staring at us. They were yelling, though we could not make out the words.

It was a fatal mistake to attempt crossing the river at that angle. Perhaps Acts Quickly or his father knew this danger. But Anna and I were panicked and desperate to escape. The main channel of the river was in the middle and its violent streams were bared by the lack of tide water. Waves bucked the surface of the torrent. The bow dipped and buried into the water. The boat jerked broadside and capsized. We were catapulted towards the nearing shore and plunged into the far edge of the main channel. The icy water stunned me. I landed on my back and the robes of my habit provided a brief buoyancy. Everything was a blur as I floated on the top of the water. I could see the shore passing by at an alarming speed. I turned my head and screamed for Anna. The clothes she was wearing had filled with water. Her head was above water and she shrieked in terror. Then she sank. I flailed my arms wildly and flipped on my stomach. I reached the spot where I last saw Anna and searched under the water for her. At last, my fingers grabbed her hair. I yanked and swam with all my might towards the shore. My habit was soaked, and the weight was pulling me under when my feet touched the muddy bottom. I was gasping as I dragged Anna up onto the sand bank. We had drifted several hundred yards down the river and the men were standing on the far side watching. Anna was not breathing. No matter how I tried, she did not regain consciousness. A cold bitter wave washed over my soul as I gazed at her beauty in death. Rage overcame me, and I ran to edge of the sand, shrieking and shaking my fist at the men on the far side. They stood aghast for a moment and then hurriedly retreated up the bluff. They glanced back as if they had the devil at their heels and disappeared into the fort.

I don't remember much after that. Anna was petite and light. Somehow, I dragged and carried her to Father Juvenal's remote cabin hidden in the woods beyond the southern riverbank. She lay on the table. Her countenance was so peaceful that I calmed down in my exhaustion and fell asleep while sitting beside her. I vowed to her that I would avenge her death. I don't know how many hours or days passed before Acts Quickly found us. Despite his grief, he thanked me for not letting her be lost to the waters. I dared not go back to the Denaina village. The chief and his people came for Anna. Since Father Juvenal was gone, they decided to cremate Anna in their traditional way. They allowed me to dress Anna in my religious habit after I cleaned it carefully. She had wanted so deeply to become a nun and I was so deeply sorrowful for having lost her.

Acts Quickly brought me my traveling bag and I put on my white dress, but I did not dance in merriment as I had once dreamed of doing in innocence. He brought me food and supplies. He cut wood for the stove and hauled water. He brought me a rifle that must have cost many furs. He showed me the waterways across the flats in his skin boat. He taught me the trails along the bluff and into the wild woods beyond.

After several weeks, Acts Quickly arrived on the tide with news of Father Juvenal. The priest had returned to the village and was horrified at the news of Anna and me. He went to the fort to demand justice for Anna. Acts Quickly's face was grim when he explained that the chief had gone to the fort to see why the monk did not return to the village, and the Russians had claimed that Father Juvenal hastened to Tyonek across the inlet to look for the women, because he hadn't believed the Denaina story about Anna's death. The chief retreated from the fort and avoided the Russians who now drank and fell into chaos.

Spring turned into summer. I longed to see Father Juvenal and waited for him in vain. I wandered the paths south along the bluffs, sometimes to the north bank of the Kasilof. One morning, a ship was anchored offshore. A skiff lay on the beach below the bluff since the tide had gone out. I spied from behind the trees on the bluff and did not hear the four men come up behind me. They were more startled than I was. "Dios!" they cried, as they caught sight of me and crossed themselves. They were Spaniards.

Despite extreme difficulty in broken English, the Spaniards and I were able to share our tales. Their leader was Captain Ignacio Aretga. The rich banker in St. Petersburg had gotten word to the Spanish King Charles the Fourth to send a rescue vessel if the English explorer Vancouver did not help me escape to Europe. The request sparked the curiosity of the Spanish royals and Captain Aretga was sent to verify my existence, explore the Alaskan coast, and claim it for Spain. The Captain visited the fort briefly and returned, saying that Konovalov had assured him that Father Juvenal had decided to build his mission in Tyonek and would return for the nun. Captain Aretga was discreet and did not divulge anything about me. He told me that the Russians had laughed and said that Father Juvenal left his nun with the Denaina. The Captain decided to leave me at the cabin for the moment and await the King's command on what to do in my regard. Again, I was overcome with loneliness as I watched the ship sail away, taking with it all my hopes.

It was late summer when fate smiled on me. I was weary of the constant diet of salmon and decided to harvest some clams on the beach. There was a spot to the south that was out of sight from both the Kenai and Kasilof Redoubts. I spent much time there when the tide was out. There was a deep ravine that cut through the bluff. A trail down the ravine made an easy escape from the open beach into the safety of the woods. In bliss with a basket full of clams, I was nearing the top of the ravine when a man stepped out of the brush. I had never heard of love at first sight. Later, he explained he had also been overcome with love for me in that moment. It was Salvadore Fidalgo.

My heart pounds when I recall Salvadore. He is tall and dark and handsome. Oh. My Salvadore. For a week after we first met, we walked the bluffs in the late summer breezes and talked. He spoke fluent Russian. He explained that he had been dropped off by a skiff on the beach to slip through the woods for reconnaissance of the redoubts and was stunned when he found me.

He was a spy for Spain and had come to see what the Russians were doing in the inlet. "I came to see Alaska and I found the Empress of Russia," he repeated in wonder.

He easily drew from me my entire story, for I was very lonely and anxious about Father Juvenal after he had been gone for so long. He told me about his home in Spain. I was taken by his words to the warmth of the sun and the bliss of the Mediterranean Sea, as well as the wine and fine culture of Spain. At the end of the week, he came to me, went down on one knee, and swore passionately that he would return for me in September on the Feast of the Archangel Michael by the Roman calendar. And so, I was left alone again.

Acts Quickly came every week with food or else I would have

gone mad. In my loneliness, I couldn't eat the Denaina foods and began to starve. My starvation was for company, for my newly beloved Salvadore. It was in this frame of mind, that I decided to haunt the Russians. At dusk, I slipped to the beach in my white dress. I shrieked in my lonely agony at them. My parents, Anna, Father Juvenal and Salvadore filled my longing and broke my heart. I wailed and would not go unheard. In the dark, I raced back up the trails to the cabin, which I knew by heart and could run blindly in the dark. I feared the giant brown bears that fished the sloughs of the river, but even they fled the anguished screams of my lonely heart.

September is passing. Acts Quickly has brought me news of the return of Captain Zaikov. Another priest has arrived. He is looking for Father Juvenal and has visited the village. He has persuaded Captain Zaikov to take him to Tyonek to see if Father Juvenal has built a mission there or has disappeared. I am certain that Konovalov and Balushin murdered the priest and hid his body in the vast wilderness. Acts Quickly assures me that such evil cannot go without consequence.

More importantly, Acts Quickly has spoken to the young Russian officer who arrived with Captain Zaikov. He assures me that Nicholas is not like the other men. Nicholas stands out against the corrupt nature of the Russians. Neither is he a career man like stalwart Captain Zaikov. We agree that this young man must have been sent from the St. Petersburg banker to find me, despite there being no indication from Nicholas that he is looking for anyone.

"He has a good heart and the spirit of a warrior," Acts Quickly says. He will bring him to me, and we shall find out. I will convince him to accompany me to Spain. It is but a few days until Michaelmas. I look for the Spaniards to return.

I will follow my heart and decide to abdicate to Spain. I will convert to Roman Catholicism. I will marry Salvadore Fidalgo. I will never be alone or cold or hungry again. With the help of King Charles, we will have justice for Anna and Father Juvenal. Konovalov and Balushin will pay for their crimes. The tide is highest tonight. A day is all that stands between me and my beloved. Tonight, Acts Quickly will bring me Nicholas, and I will enlist him to escort me to Spain in safety. The day after, we will set sail for Spain. My heart breaks to leave Father Juvenal, but I know he would want me to be safe and happy.

The script ended. Nicholas leapt up, his eyes blazing. "You cannot go to Spain," he exclaimed. "We will return to the fort immediately. I will take command and when Captain Zaikov returns, I will see to it that Konovalov and Balushin are sent back home in chains to stand trial for murder. Acts Quickly. Take us back now."

A long silence hung in the room. The wood in the stove crackled. Sophia shook her head. "No."

"Why?" demanded Nicholas.

"No." Sophia repeated calmly. She stepped forward. Emotion shook Nicholas. Her sunken eyes were strangely mismatched. Her cheeks were gaunt. She was skin and bones, and her golden hair hung limply to her waist with bits of moss and leaves in it. Her tattered dress was now a dull gray in the candlelight. He wanted to hold her and take her away from the cursed place, to restore her to comely health and vigor with the finest foods and wines, and seat her in the finest palace in the finest clothes. He wanted her to command him to great deeds. His Empress.

Acts Quickly advanced to her side, his hands held up in a gesture of peace. "Even if we tried to go back now, we can't. My boat can only hold two people. The tide is out, and the sloughs are impassable mud. You can't walk across the mudflats even with a lantern. It is too dangerous."

"The Tsarina and I go back when the tide is ready. I will send men for you," Nicholas countered.

It was silent again. "No." Sophia said firmly.

Nicholas' mind was racing. He studied the two faces before him. It dawned on him. There was something else they hadn't told him. "What. Tell me. What is it that keeps you from speaking."

Acts Quickly looked at the floor and then at Sophia. He moved to the door, opened it, and stood at the entrance. The storm had passed in the darkness of the night. There was a small chirp somewhere in the trees outside. The sky in the east was changing, and there was a faint promise of lightening at the edge of the heavens. The wind was calm and there were no clouds in the pale brightening sky. Despite the crisp air, it promised to be a sunny September day.

Sophia came to Nicholas and laid her hand on his arm. "We wait for Salvadore. He will come today. I know he will. Come with me to Spain, Nicholas."

Nicholas recoiled as if he was in deep pain. "No. Unless you tell me what it is that you are hiding, I say we follow my plan. We go back to the fort and put things right. We will take you back to Russia and give you the throne."

Sophia sighed deeply. "Nicholas. When the banker came to you from St. Petersburg, weren't you just turning old enough to leave the orphanage at the mission in Ropsha? You were trained for the military, but you were not an officer. You had no notion of what you were going to do for a career and worse, and you didn't know what you were going to do for money after being turned out from the orphanage. Fate smiled on you, that's what you told yourself when the banker promised you money and an officer's rank. But did the priests and the nuns tell you who you were? Did they tell you who your parents were?"

Nicholas' stomach turned. The golden cross hung heavily on his breast. How did Sophia know so much about him?

"Your father and mother served my father and mother. When

Catherine ordered the palace guard to find and kill my father, your father left the guard. He found my father and swore allegiance to him. Your father was my father's most trusted bodyguard. My father gave him a gold cross as a sign of the bond between our families before God. Your mother was my mother's maid in waiting. Your parents were executed with my parents. You were no more than a baby when you were placed into the care of the priests at the mission. Nothing was ever said, because if Catherine found out about your survival, she would have had you executed too. Our pasts are intertwined. Our fates are intertwined. Father Juvenal told me about you on the voyage over here. He told me to watch for you. He told me about the gold cross that you now wear that my father gave to your father as a sign of allegiance. He said I would know when I saw a tall, blond young man who was wiser than his years. The banker didn't tell you about your parents because he feared how you would react. He feared you would blame me for what happened to your parents. So, please, Nicholas, I need you to come with me to Spain. I need your help."

Nicholas shook his head. His thoughts rushed. He stepped outside to join Acts Quickly as he was listening intently. He glanced at Nicholas and gave a wry smile. "She needs you to protect her on the voyage to Spain."

Nicholas shook his head again. He wanted to take Sophia back to the fort and sort everything out. The other officers would know what to do about Konovalov and Balushin. Demidov had already threatened to put Konovalov in chains. They would be ready when Captain Zaikov returned. He resolved to take Sophia back. He drew the cross from under his shirt and studied it. He signed himself and turned to his Denaina companion.

"Is the tide coming back in?" he asked. "I have to get back to the fort. If Demidov and Vasilev wake up and I am missing, they will send a search party to the village. Who knows what trouble might happen?"

"Let's go see," replied Acts Quickly. He led the way into the woods. They left the knoll and made their way to the edge of the bluff directly across from the far bank where the fort stood. They paused a moment, studying the waters off the beach. It seemed Acts Quickly was watching the fort as if he were waiting for something to happen. The tide had just turned, and it would be hours before it reached the river and filled the sloughs.

"The water is low in the sloughs. I can make it back to my village in the boat if only I am in it," Acts Quickly spoke decisively. He continued, "The Russians have brought evil here. They don't listen to their own priests who preach love and kindness and sharing. They have done too many bad things." As Acts Quickly spoke, there was a deep sadness in his voice.

Nicholas was shaken within himself as his heart sank at the words of the chief's son.

Acts Quickly continued steadfastly, "My father has prepared for war, to attack the fort and drive the Russians out of our lands forever. He will avenge my sister and all the offended spirits of Yaghanen."

Acts Quickly put a firm hand on Nicholas' shoulder. "You were born to protect Princess Sophia. Stay with her and protect her in Spain. There is nothing for you here now." He flashed a smile and turned to leave. Nicholas stared after him as Acts Quickly melted into the trees like a shadow, tall and full of purpose.

TEN

THE MORNING PROGRESSED SLOWLY. The sun rose reluctantly in a blood red sky. The far mountains puffed steam as if the scent of death and violence was filling the air. An apprehensive hush fell over the land. All the birds hid and refused to greet the day with joyful songs. The quiet was heavy and ominous. A stench rose from the great flats of the river delta, a foulness that had not spread in the previous weeks. The putrid smells of dead beach grass and rotting salmon carcasses mingled dreadfully on the stifling heavy air.

Acts Quickly found his way across the sloughs and the river currents to the familiar beach of the village. The village was still. There were no dogs running out and barking in greeting the chief's son. There were no cries of hungry babies waking. No children stirred outside. He pulled the boat up and ran to his house. His mother had been waiting by the door and watching anxiously for him. She smoothed the hair on his forehead and touched his shoulders. She did not hug him. She did not want to distract her son from the grim task ahead of him. Her dark eyes were full of emotion, pride mingled with terror and resignation to her son's initiation in to battle. Tears welled at the corners of her eyes.

"Son." The chief spoke firmly.

He was sitting at the wooden table. He had been cleaning two rifles and pistols. He readied the pouches of gunpowder and musket bullets.

The large knives were shining on the table with razor sharp blades. "These Spanish rifles are better than the Russian ones. They don't rust. They shoot straighter and are faster to load with gunpowder. They are lighter too."

The chief held a rifle up admiringly. "These rifles will help us fight well today."

"Eat, son." The chief leaned the rifles by the door and cleared the table off. His wife set mugs of tea down with bowls of stew. The three of them ate in anxious silence. Acts Quickly noticed his mother hardly touched her food. She rose to clear the dishes as the men went to the door. The day had just begun to break. A reddish gray light filled the sky. The men of the village emerged from their houses and assembled in the yard of the chief's house. Women and children stood in the doorways, peering at their men in silence. The men gathered in a throng holding their rifles with knives and gunpowder pouches in their belts. Some men had bows slung across their backs with quivers of sharp tipped arrows.

Spear lumbered up with the great bear skin rolled up and secured with sinews. He heaved it into the middle of the yard with a grunt. Chuckles rippled through the gathering. There were twenty young men who were the same age as Acts Quickly, with some slightly older and a few who were younger but large for their age. They arrived carrying piles of dried seal and otter pelts that were tied together in bundles.

The last arrival was the elder of the village, wrapped in a caribou blanket and assisted by his great grandsons on each arm. The elder's hair was long and white upon his shoulders. He squinted up at the sky and was silent for a long moment. He motioned for the bear hide, which was immediately placed at his feet. The elder softly sang a song.

Acts Quickly glanced at his father. He remembered that his father had told him once that these songs had no age because they were too old for memory. The Ts'itsatna, the ancient ones, sang these songs and handed them down generation after generation. He briefly wondered how many elders before them had sung the song, and how many generations of Kahtnuht'ana had bravely faced war in the same manner of the men before him now. He thought of the giant in the story his father had told the Russians, and how brave the men were who dispatched the evil intruder without fear. He smiled inwardly as he recognized that his father had told the Russians the story to warn them that in their greed and cruelty, they had become the giant and needed to be killed for the safety of the Kahtnuht'ana, the people of the river flats.

Acts Quickly recalled Ada, his sister. His heart hurt. She was a good sister. She was beautiful. She had nursed the sick and helped watch little children. She was quick to help elders. Acts Quickly thought of how all the villagers had loved her and as he gazed around, he knew that everyone still loved her and missed her as he did. He knew the village stood as one to fight in her memory and drive the evil Russians out before any more women were destroyed by them. Acts Quickly's hand gripped his rifle tighter and he stood taller. Today, Acts Quickly was a warrior.

The fort cook had overslept. He roused himself at last and mumbled in complaint as he crossed the yard from his bunk, blinking drowsily as he surveyed the red sky. It could only mean a bad omen.

"This looks like a bad day *already*," the cook muttered to himself.

To his immense relief, the officers' quarters were silent. The sound of heavy breathing from upstairs drifted down as he let himself in and gingerly set to lighting the cook stove. The cook took his time brewing the coffee and tiptoed as he gathered pans to cook. The officers were still asleep. An hour later, the aroma of baking bread awakened the men upstairs. Demidov sleepily descended the stairs. When Vasilev followed, the men settled at the table for their morning coffee.

"Where is our youngest officer? Where is Nicholas?" Vasilev inquired.

Demidov frowned. "Hopefully, he is outside in the yard. I told the men not to go outside the fort until it is time to work, so they would be protected by an armed guard." He stepped out. A moment later, Demidov reentered and strode upstairs.

Vasilev heard Demidov rousing Konovalov to ask him if he knew where the Nicholas had gone. Konovalov groaned sleepily in reply and said that he had slept deeply for the first time in ages and hadn't heard any noises. He did not know where the young man was.

"Get up, then. Eat your breakfast and join work today. Act like a commanding officer should," Demidov scolded.

Demidov returned downstairs leaving Konovalov to stiffly struggle out of bed. He sat down at the table uneasily and addressed Vasilev. "His bed doesn't look slept in. Where is Nicholas? We don't need more trouble. I don't want a confrontation with those natives now. First, Konovalov acting crazy and sick in bed, now Nicholas is missing, I feel like a child's nurse."

Vasilev soothed his fellow officer. "Let's eat and then take a good look around the fort. Nicholas is young. He is unmarried and restless. Surely, he is just near the fort, or maybe even looking at the skiff he found the other day. There must be a good explanation. If not, we can put together some armed men and go down to the native village and look for him there. He is a levelheaded serious boy. I am sure he is fine. Stay patient, Demidov. Zaikov will be back before you know, and we will sail home." He eyed Konovalov who limped down the stairs and lowered himself in a chair. Vasilev winked at Demidov.

The officers ate in silence. The cook sat near the stove, stuffing a piece of wood inside it every now and then. Konovalov sipped his coffee and nibbled at a piece of bread. His face was purplish and swollen. The tense meal finally came to an unsatisfactory end.

Demidov stood and resolutely pushed his chair back. "Let's search for Nicholas." As he reached for the door, it was yanked open, and he started back in surprise.

It was Igor. "The natives are at the gate." He peered in the doorway, spied Konovalov, and nodded a greeting.

Demidov turned back and frowned at Vasilev, exasperated by yet another challenge presenting itself so early in the day.

Igor continued, "The natives have piles of furs they want to trade. A man killed that medved that attacked us the other night. It went to the village after we chased it off. He says he killed it with a spear. He has brought the hide to show us. It is all tied up, but it is so big, he can barely carry it. It's the biggest bear hide I have ever seen. He is going to spread it out and show the men."

Vasilev stood up and asked, "Why didn't the dogs bark? I didn't hear any warning that people came to the gate."

Igor nodded his big head stupidly. "The boy had meat. He gave some to the dogs at the gate. The chief's son." He leaned in, but Demidov pushed him firmly back.

"How are you?" The giant directed his question to Konovalov.

Konovalov shook his head. "I am going to lie down again. I don't feel like I can work today." He shuffled towards the stairs.

Demidov closed the door on Igor and turned towards Vasilev. "This day is starting to look better. Let's see about these furs the natives brought to trade." Vasilev grinned broadly and joined him at the door.

They both knew Zaikov would be pleased if they presented him with a load of precious furs to take back to Russia when he returned from Tyonek. A small investment of the glass trade beads brought from Russia in exchange for a bounty of furs would surely delight the Captain. They did not need to assemble an armed search party and venture to the village to locate Nicholas. They could ask the natives right in their own yard if they had seen him since last night. The day suddenly looked brighter.

The officers stepped onto the shabby porch of the quarters. They were shocked to see fifty Denaina men in the center of the yard. Demidov exchanged a wide-eyed glance with Vasilev. The village men had each brought a large bundle of furs which they laid in great stacks. Vasilev gave a giggle. The Denaina men set their burdens down and sat next to the piles. Demidov recognized one of the young men from the previous night as a companion to the chief. Spear was heaving the bear hide on the ground and sat on it as he wiped sweat from his brow. The Russians streamed from their barracks and gathered around the Denaina. The fort dogs wagged their tails as they sought a pat on the head from the generous Denaina who had brought delicious bites of meat.

Spear surveyed the gathering Russians and yelled in his Denaina language, "I, Spear, I killed the bear that tried to break into your redoubt. I shot him with an arrow and finished him with a lance. This bear is the largest bruin that our people have memory of. Our elders looked at it and said they had never seen any bear so large. I will show you."

Acts Quickly stood and translated. The Russians continued pouring into the compound and crowding around Spear.

Gregori Konovalov stirred and cocked his head. He heard loud voices emanating from the yard. He sat up and strained his ears.

He realized it was the sound of several hundred men. Konovalov forgot his ulcer and gave in to his swelling curiosity as he jammed his feet in his boots and staggered down the stairs. He cracked the door and peeked past the backs of Demidov and Vasilev in front of him on the porch. Igor was looming over the young Denaina man they called Spear, while other Russians behind him shoved each other to get a view from behind. He caught the last of Acts Quickly's words about the bear and strained to see the monster's hide as it was laid across the ground. He dared not venture outside and face the ire of Demidov.

Spear scanned the men crowded around him now. He smiled teasingly. All eyes transfixed on him as he slowly rose from sitting without turning, his muscular legs pulling him up steadily. He flexed his arms as if he were bored. He carefully reached for the rope that bound the hide in a roll and tugged on it, taunting the men. He fiddled with it a long moment before pulling it free. The roll of hide opened a bit. An impatient murmur ran through the men. Within the next second, there was only a collective gasp. The men were frozen in terror.

In a flash, Spear kicked open the hide, whipped up a lance and jumping high into the air, stabbed Igor in the left eye. A scream of rage burst from Spears' lips, a war call to his brother warriors to begin the attack. As the Russians stared in disbelief, Igor groaned and fell forward onto the bear hide, impaling the spear through the eye socket and out the back of his skull. He twitched once and lay still.

The Russians all stood in frozen shock. The chief barked an order and like a flash of lightning, the Denaina men reached into their bundles of hides to pull out the knives and Spanish rifles. The chief leaped up and aimed his rifle. Demidov was opening his mouth to yell a command when a musket ball hit him in the forehead. He fell off the porch with a puff of dirt rising where he hit the ground.

Vasilev reached for his pistol and raised it, but was too late. The chief had sprung up onto the porch and struck Vasilev with his rifle butt. Vasilev staggered back a step, his weight banging the door shut. The chief was on the attack and in an instant, unsheathed his knife and slit Vasilev's throat before he could recover his balance. Inside the door, Konovalov fell back onto the floor. His chest heaved as he gasped. He didn't think the chief had seen him peeking out of the door, but he wasn't sure. In a panic, he slid backwards behind the stove and cowered for his life.

The Russians in the yard were all paralyzed by the instantaneous violence. The men in the center of the yard were trapped by rings of men behind them. The dogs began growling and snapping to attack anyone who was nearby. The Denaina men calmly raised their muskets and fired. The closest Russian men fell, dying instantly from point blank shots. The men nearest to the gate stampeded out. They were met with arrows from the bows of another fifty Denaina men hidden in the bushes surrounding the fort. The mayhem had only begun.

THE FORT COOK HAD BEEN IN THE SUPPLY SHED after making the morning coffee, trying to assess how much flour was left. Hearing a commotion in the yard, he peeked through the slats in the shed to see the cause of the ruckus. He watched in horror as the attack unfolded. When the cook saw the fall of officers, his heart filled with indignation. He saw the men fleeing towards the gate. He glanced to the side of the shed. There stood the rifles waiting to be cleaned. He swept one up and loaded a musket ball and gunpowder in a flash. The cook kicked open the shed door and yelled in Russian. He lifted the rifle and aimed. Spear fell. Spear's body landed on top of Igor as blood gushed from the side of his head. The cook yelled again. His fellow men heard him and rushed to the shed for the rifles. A throng of Russians gathered behind the shed. The cook and another man threw guns and ammunition out as fast as they could. The rifles were passed, and men loaded the shot behind the shed. The cook jumped out and yelled, "Aim. Fire." Denaina men fell.

The cook had begun to yell orders for his riflemen behind the shed to reload, when a man grabbed his arm. "Let's get the rifles and ammunition out of the fort. Let us go to the wood pile and make a stand. We can barricade the natives inside and burn them."

Without considering, the cook agreed. The men swiftly loaded their rifles and streamed out the gate, firing at the native archers.

In the close confines of the yard, the fighting was no longer with rifles. Knives and hand to hand combat erupted. The Russians were taller and outweighed the Denaina men. The fighting was fierce and bloody. The Russians grabbed any stick, log, or piece of iron within reach to swing against the slashing knives of the quick Denaina. The men fought viciously as many fell in death at a furious rate.

"LET'S GET UP THERE," LAST WATERS URGED Acts Quickly, as he pulled on the chief's son's arm to duck under the porch of the officers' quarters, out of the way of an axe-swinging Russian.

Last Waters' eye was swollen shut from a glancing blow of a metal rod. "If we get upstairs and punch the windows out, we can shoot down on them."

Acts Quickly nodded. He spied several rifles and pouches of bullets on a pile of pelts nearby. He crawled towards the rifles and soon had them under his arm. Acts Quickly glanced around to find his father. He caught sight of him near the porch, bending over a fallen Russian. "Father," Acts Quickly cried and ran to his side, pulling the chief up onto the porch and inside the quarters. Last Waters was already inside. He grabbed the rifles from Acts Quickly and dashed up the stairs. Acts Quickly and his father slid the table against the door and threw the chairs on top. They raced upstairs. Last Waters had ripped open the windows overlooking the yard outside and was loading the rifles as fast as he could. Acts Quickly seized a rifle and aimed.

BEHIND THE COOK STOVE ON THE FIRST LEVEL, Konovalov had covered himself with pieces of wood and lay still. He heard the native men enter. Terror swept over the Russian. His stomach turned and his legs were frozen while his mind raced in thoughts of what he should do. After hearing the rifles discharging out the upstairs windows, Konovalov decided that he should merely continue to do what was keeping him safe. The natives did not know he was hiding behind the stove. He planned to remain hidden until the fighting died down. Then he would sneak out. Konovalov wondered what he would do once he was outside. The skiff floated into his mind. He knew what he would do. He would take the skiff to Kasilof and get help. Konovalov relaxed and waited.

ELEVEN

NICHOLAS SAT EMOTIONLESS IN THE CABIN. His mind was numb. Sophia was sitting at the door of the tiny room, listening. She glanced at him from time to time. Her face was expressionless and neither of them attempted to speak. It seemed that dawn would never arrive. Sophia's words rang in his mind. Her Spaniards had sold the Denaina men rifles for furs and some gold nuggets. The rifles had arrived in the skiff he had found on the beach. The Spanish vessel was somewhere in the inlet, hiding from view. The young man's mind was a storm of thoughts. When Acts Quickly told him about the Denaina attack on the fort, he feared that the Russians would slaughter the men only armed with bows and spears. Now that he knew the Denaina had rifles, he feared for Demidov and Vasilev. The men had families in Russia. The two officers were looking forward to going home to Russia on the St. George.

Nicholas felt sick. He closed his eyes. An image appeared in his mind. It was unbidden and he was startled. It was his father. A memory where his father stood tall in uniform, with a stern face and a gold cross shining on his breast.

Nicholas opened his eyes. He studied the ghost of a woman across the room. He thought of the terror the men at the fort felt from her haunting. Several hours passed in the stillness. The daylight finally arrived, and the interior of the cabin brightened.

"You knew my father?" Nicholas asked.

Sophia turned from the door and answered, "Yes. He was very serious. But your mother was very kind. She was very beautiful and gentle. Not at all like your father."

Nicholas burst out passionately, "You are NOT Rusalka. Konovalov is wrong. The men at the fort are wrong."

Sophia started. She pondered the Nicholas' words a while before speaking. "Is that what they say I am?" She laughed. "Perhaps I was Rusalka for a time. Then I met Salvadore, and I realized that I do not want to be Rusalka anymore."

THE BATTLE AT THE FORT RAGED FOR HOURS. Acts Quickly, Last Waters and his father ran out of ammunition for the rifles. They descended the stairs and returned outside to the yard after pulling the table and chairs from the door. The Russians now held the area near the shed and the remaining Denaina fighters were staged around the officers' quarters. Corpses of the fallen were strewn across the yard, along with carcasses of dogs and torn pelts. Wounded men moaned as they lay dying on the edges of the yard. The stench of death, gunpowder, sweat, and fresh human blood hung over the fort.

The men, both Russian and Denaina, now paused a moment and fell back to their separate positions. If men ventured forth to rescue a wounded companion, the other fighters would rally and attack in a charge. Both sides would meet again in the center of the yard and fight until more men fell, before withdrawing back to their corner. It was a ghastly dance of war.

AFTER THE CHIEF AND HIS NEPHEW AND SON had left the quarters, Konovalov stirred from behind the stove. He crept to the door and surveyed the yard. The Denaina were holding their spot around the quarters, so he feared leaving the front door. He thought for a moment. He decided he could crawl out the upstairs window and onto the roof over the back of the building. He hoped to leap onto the wall of the fort and crawl to the bluff through the bushes. Konovalov closed the door and began to climb the stairs.

THE CHIEF STOOD BEHIND THE OFFICERS' QUARTERS. He turned to Acts Quickly and Last Waters. "Konovalov must be hiding in the shed over there. I haven't seen him. Have you?"

Acts Quickly and Last Waters each shook their heads. The chief spit the words out, "I will kill him, for he is the commander of the fort and the man responsible for my daughter's death. When the Russians see him dead, they will be defeated and surrender. We will let those who surrender leave on the ship to their homeland." Acts Quickly and Last Waters nodded in unison.

The chief continued, "I will tell the men to charge, and we will all spread out. You two will come with me and go along the side of the fort to attack the shed in the rear. We will storm it, find Konovalov, and kill him."

Acts Quickly tightened his grip around his knife. The chief called the men together and shared his plan. The men readied themselves and at the chief's yell, rushed forward.

The few Russians that remained alive in the fort had stepped forward to drag several of their wounded men to the shed for cover. They straightened in surprise to meet the charge. Acts Quickly darted behind his father along the wall with Last Waters at his heels. They reached the shed easily and unnoticed.

KONOVALOV PULLED HIMSELF OUT OF THE WINDOW and grasped the edge of the roof. For a moment, he hung precariously on the precipice. He looked down. The chief and two young men were running along the wall below him. In fear, he swung his leg up and gained the roof. Konovalov paused a moment to study the fort wall for a place to grab on to when he jumped off from the top. His stomach turned as he doubted himself. He would fall into the yard and be injured. He knew the chief meant to kill him. He knew he was the reason the natives attacked the fort. He thought of Anna. He thought of the ghost and terror seized him. *Whatever will be, will be.*

THE COOK STOOD AT THE WOOD PILE. On his left and right were five Russians. "The ammunition is used up, but the archers are all shot. We must get back in that shed and get more bullets."

The cook looked at the men who nodded. "We charge in and grab the supplies and charge out. Go."

The Russian men raced back to the fort.

There were two Russian men cowering behind the shed. The chief's knife slashed swiftly, and the men fell. The chief leapt inside the shed. Acts Quickly followed. Last Waters hesitated to guard the door.

When their eyes adjusted to the shadows of the shed, the chief observed, "Konovalov isn't here." Acts Quickly moved a bag. "There's more gunpowder and bullets."

The chief looked pleased. "Take it back to the quarters. Our rifles are still upstairs." They filled their arms and stepped out.

A shot rang out. The chief grunted and fell. The cook stood just inside the gate with a rifle. Acts Quickly screamed, "Father!" as he threw himself across the fallen chief. Last Waters leapt. Last Water's knife flashed and the cook slumped to the ground.

Last Waters yelled, "Take him to the quarters, Acts Quickly!"

Last Waters gave a spine-chilling cry that all the Denaina knew as the rallying cry of a fallen chief in battle, and their enemies knew as the sound heralding a horrific change in pitch of the battle. As Acts Quickly heaved his father on his shoulders and raced to the quarters, he saw Last Waters fighting more fiercely than any man had ever fought. The young warrior feigned, stabbed, jumped, and slashed. The cook's men fell in death one by one as they tried to stop the young man. The last surviving Russian noticed the eye was swollen shut on one side of Last Water's face. The Russian feinted a step sideways before he attacked the vulnerable blind side, taking advantage of the Denaina's obstructed vision. Last Waters fell.

KONOVALOV SPRANG FROM THE ROOF AT THE SOUND of a bloodcurdling scream. He cleared the wall and landed heavily on the outside. He groaned. A small stick was embedded in his thigh and the breath was knocked out of him. When he had regained his breath, the Russian scanned his surroundings furtively. He yanked the stick from his thigh and cursed vehemently in his desperation. No one was in sight. He crawled towards the bluff.

WHEN THE SKY HAD LIGHTENED WITH BLOOD RED STREAKS, Sophia stirred. Without speaking, she pulled on her tattered dingy fur coat and stepped outside. Nicholas followed. She wandered along a trail from the cabin. It was strangely and ominously quiet. The pair hiked for a time as the morning progressed. After a while, the trail turned out at the top of the bluff. The land before them expanded along the flats of the delta of the great Kenai River. Beyond the flats and the river rose the bluff with the redoubt on its crest. It was so far away; the redoubt was merely a shadow. To the west, a puff of steam rose from the mountain top across the inlet.

Sophia crossed herself. She murmured a prayer for the success and safety of her friend, Acts Quickly and his Denaina people.

After a long moment of silence, she turned to Nicholas. "The Denaina should be in the fort by now." Nicholas frowned.

Sophia continued, "The plan was to hide the rifles that the Spanish provided in bundles of fur. The men from the village would gain access to the inside of the fort under the pretense of trading furs. The greed for the furs will make the Russians at the fort drop their guard. The Denaina men are fewer, but they will have the element of surprise and they are sober and more cunning fighters than the Russians. They will be fighting for their women and children and their lands."

"I know the 'Russians' as you put it, Sophia. I am one of them. I just spent weeks with Demidov and Vasilev on board the St. George. They are trying to fix things at the fort. They are good men. Good officers. Husbands and fathers." Nicholas spoke in confused anger.

"No." Sophia shook her head vehemently. "Nyet. Nicholas, you are not one of those men. You are not a company man. Those men are greedy. All they care about is money. Money from furs and goods taken from these people, these Denaina people."

Her eyes blazed with emotion. "These men and their company are destroying the Denaina people. I have seen it with my own eyes."

"Then come back to Russia with me. Take the throne and make things right," Nicholas argued.

Sophia shook her head. "Nyet. No, Nicholas. This fight is not mine. I have lost everything. Everything. I have starved and haunted this godforsaken place. But, despite all things and against all odds, I was blessed with love. *If you are given something, take it. If you are being beaten, run.* Didn't the priests teach that proverb to you in the monastery? The nuns taught me. I am not running, Nicholas. I have been given something. I have been given hope where there is no hope. I have hope of a new life in a sunny warm paradise far from here, where there is only cold death. I will take it.

"What would happen if I did go back to Russia? What do you think, Nicholas? First, I would have to prove I am the rightful heir to the throne. Then, I would have to vanquish not only Catherine the Great, but I would have to begin a blood bath by eliminating all her loyal subjects. How do you think she became Catherine the Great? It is because she has power, power over men who will kill for her. That is only the beginning. She has studied the philosophies of Voltaire and put in place changes in our Russian traditions and society that are no longer based on principle or beliefs, but on the so-called Enlightenment of Man. She has wielded her power to undermine the Church, the priests, aristocracy, and our noble royal history. Look at me, Nicholas. I am that aristocracy, that religion, that history. I loved and obeyed the nuns and the priests. I can never forget their kindness to me, an orphan. It is because of Father Juvenal that I am even alive. How can I turn against the institution that saved me?"

Sophia slumped and buried her head in her hands. She moaned, "I am done, Nicholas. I am worn out. I am that ghost that haunts. Nothing of me is left, but one tiny hope that the Spanish will come, and I will leave this place forever."

Nicholas saw her pale skin stretched over bones, the ragged dress and tattered fur coat and shuddered. He felt old beyond his years, a weariness of his mission to bring back the woman. He felt the hopelessness of the filthy fort and the destruction of the Denaina and their women. She looked up at him. Her eyes still shone with the remains of a royal beauty that had been starved away in the wilderness. Her words stabbed his young passionate heart, and he melted.

"I need you, Nicholas. I need you to accompany me to Spain."

He stood a long moment staring at the fort far away on the bluff before going down on a knee and answering gruffly, "I will never leave your side, my Tsarina. I will always serve you." Nicholas drew a deep breath and resigned himself to accompany his Tsarina to Spain. He would serve her as long as she needed him. He took her hands in his own and squeezed them tightly.

ACTS QUICKLY SET HIS FATHER ON THE TABLE of the officers' quarters as softly as he could. He pulled back the chief's leather shirt and inspected the wound. The bullet had gone through the man's shoulder and exited through the back. It appeared that the shot was a flesh wound and had missed the bones and lungs. Blood was still gushing out to his alarm. Acts Quickly glanced around the kitchen and spied a bottle of vodka on one of the shelves. He recalled watching his sister Anna nurse a wounded villager. She had carefully cleaned the wound with vodka before bandaging it with a clean cloth. Acts Quickly swept up the vodka and scooped some chinking out of the logs on the walls of the quarters. He hastily poured the liquid in the wound and applied the chinking. His father moaned and fell silent. Acts Quickly found a towel and pressed it over the wound. He paused a moment, trying to gather his thoughts. Acts Quickly gathered his father up again to carry him upstairs to a bed. After settling his father as comfortably as he could, Acts Quickly stood another moment. The window on the back wall was torn open. Acts Quickly crossed the room and looked out.

A wind was rising and whistling into the open frame of the window. Acts Quickly drew a deep breath and noticed the salty air. It was the wind that blew in with the high tide. He listened. The din of the battle had died down. The few men that remained alive had paused in a standoff on each side of the fort, with the native men taking guard of the officers' quarters to protect their chief. Acts Quickly thought a moment. Where was Konovalov? He was not cowering in the quarters and had not been in the shed either. The skiff and its tiny white sail flashed in Acts Quickly's mind, and he knew that the coward Konovalov was trying to flee.

THERE WAS A LOW WHISTLE ECHOING in the forests behind Nicholas and Sophia.

Sophia started, stared at Nicholas, then stepped onto the trail leading back to the cabin. "Salvadore is here."

TWELVE

CAPTAIN STEPHAN ZAIKOV GRASPED THE ROPE ladder and held it steady with one hand while he guided the Russian Orthodox priest with the other. The Russians' business in Tyonek was accomplished earlier than expected, and it was time to leave. The landing skiff gently rocked and banged against the stolid wooden timbers of the massive vessel, St. George. Zaikov watched as the priest topped the deck railing and began climbing aboard his ship. Father Ioasaf stood waiting for the Captain on deck. Zaikov strode to the helm as the men saluted him with the priest falling in behind him at his heels. He barked an order as the crew began to hoist bundles of fur, baskets of meat, and boxes of wood for cooking on board. He ordered a crew man to accompany Amos Balushin immediately to his quarters, commanding to not let him out.

Father Iosaf stood silently. The native people of Tyonek had warily welcomed the Russians. The redoubt was in somewhat better shape than the fort of St. Nicholas in Kenay. There was a small church that had been built, and a few dozen natives attended liturgy when Father Iosaf celebrated the Sunday worship. After a few days, that the elder of the Tyonek village and his wife came to the priest for a visit. They sipped tea and nibbled biscuits. Father Iosaf had asked them if they knew anything of the whereabouts of Father Juvenal.

The Tyonek elder spoke slowly and related everything. Months before, Father Juvenal had sailed to Tyonek. Father Juvenal was upset that the Kahtnuht'ana chief's daughter had drowned. Gregori Konovalov had caused her death and the priest wanted to have the guilty fort commander sent back to Russia to stand trial. Father Juvenal was heartbroken over the event, and feared the Denaina people would reject the Orthodox mission because of the ill treatment they received at the fort. After some time, Father Juvenal became very close to the Tyonek elder and his wife. He was curious about their history and that of other native cultures in the area. One day, the Tyonek elder was happily sharing hunting stories, when he told the priest about the great Kuskokwim River to the north of the mountains. This information captured the priest's attention. Father Juvenal asked endless questions and became passionate about spreading the Good News with the natives along the Kuskokwim. Father Juvenal took two young men from Tyonek and left to the land in the north and east to find the people of the Kuskokwim and claim their souls for the Christ. There had been no word or news of the Father Juvenal's venture.

The Tyonek elder's account left Father Iosaf with little left to do but to return to Russia and gather more priests for the missions in Alaska. Father Iosaf had shared the news with Captain Zaikov, who assured him that a church and mission buildings would be built by the time of his return from Russia to the St. Nicholas Redoubt. Captain Zaikov was pleased with the furs and supplies he had gathered at Tyonek. He was eager to load the St. George and return to Kenay briefly. before turning his sails home towards Russia and leaving behind the deadly Alaskan winter squalls.

Acts Quickly leapt from the roof like a lynx. He cleared the fort wall. Acts Quickly jumped up and sprinted towards the path leading down the bluff to the beach. When he reached the bottom of the hill, Acts Quickly spied the man he was hunting.

Konovalov was moaning as he loosened the mooring rope. He waded chest-deep into the tide as he pushed the skiff further from the shore. He glanced up at the trail and froze as he saw Acts Quickly. Konovalov's heart seized in his breast. The tide lapped at his chest as he gripped the bow of the skiff.

"Konovalov." Acts Quickly stood on the bank above the Russian. He yanked the pistol from his belt and pointed it at the man below him.

After Anna had died and her body was buried, the chief and his son had gone trapping. They caught a pair of wolves. The fur was the finest they had seen. The Denaina chief had brought the furs to Konovalov and insisted on trading for pistols in return for such excellent quality of wolf hide. Konovalov had laughed and sent them back home empty handed. Acts Quickly and his father then traveled to the redoubt in Kasilof. There, they easily obtained pistols and ammunition. Acts Quickly and his father returned home. The pistols were for the men who killed Anna.

Acts Quickly spoke in Denaina.

"I can't understand you. I don't speak Denaina!" Konovalov cried out.

"My sister Anna. You and Belushin killed her," Acts Quickly yelled back in Russian.

Konovalov now sobbed. "I am sorry. I didn't mean for her to drown. I liked her. She was beautiful. I am sorry. I was drunk. I am sorry."

Acts Quickly reached into the pouch around his waist. He drew out a gold cross and held it high by the chain. It was the one given to his sister by Father Juvenal. Konovalov stared. The gold glinted in the sun as the cross swung in the gusts of wind. The glare blinded the Russian and he screamed lowering his head. Acts Quickly's blood boiled at the sight of the simpering man below him. Another gust of wind blew and swung the cross again.

"*Acts Quickly. I am Anna. Let me go. Forgive him. Let him go. Don't kill him to avenge me. I am free.*" It was the whisper of words in the wind and the blinding glare of the swaying burnished cross that filled Acts Quickly's heart.

Acts Quickly's hand shook a moment as it gripped the pistol with the barrel aimed at Konovalov's head.

Konovalov braced and wept. He screamed as the pistol shot cracked. It took the Russian a moment to realize he had not been shot. He opened his eyes and looked up. Acts Quickly was gone. Konovalov dove in the boat and grabbed the oars in an instant. He rowed furiously against the tide and across the river away from the beach and the fort above. He did not dare to look back at the bluff. If he had, he would have seen the tall young Kahtnuht'ana man, Acts Quickly, standing on the top of the bluff like a sturdy, enduring spruce tree in the afternoon sun, as it began its descent from the red tinted sky.

SOPHIA RACED ALONG THE TRAIL LIKE A WRAITH floating through the forest. Nicholas hurried to keep up with her. When they reached the cabin, they found two men waiting. They wore Spanish military uniforms. The tallest Spaniard turned at the sound of Sophia's running with a bemused air before both men grabbed their rifles and took a stance at the sight of Nicholas. The well-kept rifles shone with a dangerous glint in the sunlight.

"Salvadore. You have come like you promised." Sophia was

breathless. "This is Nicholas. He is my bodyguard. His father was my father's bodyguard."

The men lowered their rifles and exchanged a glance. Salvadore Fidalgo stepped forward from the cabin towards the Tsarina. He was tall, well-dressed man in an immaculate uniform, with long dark hair and a groomed beard. His eyes were wary as he surveyed Nicholas. Nicholas met the Spaniard's eyes. He could see strength and cunning in the man, but there was something more. It was kindness.

"We must go now. The tide is right. We must hurry to the skiff." Salvadore spoke urgently in perfect Russian. "Get your things."

"Nicholas is the son of my father's royal guard. He has sailed from Russia to get me and bring me back to Russia," Sophia said. She raised a hand to stop Salvadore as the Spaniard stepped forward, shaking his head. "Listen, Salvadore! It is fate! The banker from St. Petersburg arranged for Nicholas to be trained and receive an officer's commission on Captain Zaikov's boat. The banker sent Nicholas as a backup plan because he lost contact with Father Juvenal. The banker did not know about you, Salvadore. He feared I was dead, but sent Nicholas to find me. Nicholas's fate is intertwined with mine. His father swore to protect my father and my family. And so it is. Nicholas will accompany me to Spain. He will serve me as his father did. Nicholas cannot go back to Russia. He will be killed." Sophia spoke with such authority that Salvadore stepped back and nodded kindly to Nicholas.

Sophia hurriedly entered the cabin and grabbed the bag she had already packed. Salvadore's companion took the bag from her and waited. The two Spaniards, Nicholas, and Sophia took a last look at the cabin before stepping along the trail to the south.

Acts Quickly walked the trail back to the fort with a sure gait. He had watched the skiff with Konovalov drift across the delta of the river where Konovalov had lifted the little sail. The pistol bullet had punctured the hull of the skiff a foot below the topside. It was just enough damage to keep Konovalov bailing water out of the little barque at a steady pace, forcing him to fight from drowning in the choppy inlet waters.

Death hung over the fort. Somewhere a dog cried in its death throes. The bodies of Russians and Denaina warriors lay around the outside of the fort and across the yard, behind and under buildings, so that there was no place to glance around the fort without seeing a dead or dying man. Acts Quickly hurried to his father. Some of the surviving Denaina men stood guard at the porch of the officers' quarters, and several were inside with his father who remained unconscious.

Acts Quickly took a trusted man with him to assess the fort. Three Russians remained alive and lay somewhere halfway between death and life near the shed. They were in no condition to fight any more. A quick walk around the outside of the fort revealed only dead bodies. Acts Quickly decided that the Denaina's fight was done. He ordered the men who were able to carry the wounded Denaina warriors back to the village to be nursed by the women and elders. Then, they would come back to the fort, gather the dead, and burn them. Acts Quickly would carry his father himself back to the village.

"WHAT THE HELL IS GOING ON?" Captain Zaikov yelled in a burst of anger. He closed the spyglass with vehemence and kicked a nearby wooden bucket. Father Iosaf clucked his tongue.

Zaikov immediately repented, "Sorry, Father. Forgive me, please." Zaikov growled.

"What is it?" the priest inquired.

Zaikov jabbed a finger towards the eastern shores of the inlet. "What is it? What is it? You tell me. It is a Spanish galleon. What is a Spanish galleon doing here?"

The Captain thrust the spyglass into the priest's hands. "See for yourself."

The priest opened the glass and braced himself on the railing of the St. George to study the shoreline. It took the priest a few minutes to find the billowing sails of the vessel in the distance. "She can't mean too much trouble. She is racing towards the open ocean."

The priest peered in the glass a moment longer. "She is a beauty. Look at her go."

The Captain grunted. He stood staring across the inlet with a deep scowl. "I was ready to go to the fort, pick up the furs, and sail home with a load of goods and enjoy the good graces of the company men. Now, there is trouble."

"Maybe they are just exploring?" countered the priest.

"Or looking for a fight," scoffed Zaikov. "Just when I thought everything was going well."

He squinted. "What the . . .?" he roughly grabbed the spyglass from the priest. He stared into the glass.

The Captain called his first officer. The man joined his side. "Tell me what you see out there along the northern coast," Zaikov ordered.

The officer held the glass to his eyes for a long minute. "I can't really tell, Captain, but it looks like a landing skiff on the water. She has her tiny sail up. Looks like she's heading south to Kasilof."

The officer handed the glass back. "Full sail ahead. We need to reach that skiff, save whoever is on board, and get back to the St. George Redoubt as quickly as possible," Zaikov ordered.

KONOVALOV WINCED AS HE PADDLED THE SKIFF. His thigh burned where the stick had punctured him during his fall from the top of the fort wall. His stomach turned and his head spun. He glanced back and decided that he was far enough from shore to stop paddling and put up the sail. The garrison commander struggled to set up the sail. At last, the breeze caught the tiny sail and the skiff launched southward towards Kasilof. There was a cold splash on the Russian's feet. To his alarm and dismay, waves had found the hole from the well-aimed pistol shot of Acts Quickly back at the beach. Tears welled up in his eyes, and he whimpered as he scanned the inlet around him. The sail had already pushed him out into the deep far from shore.

Terror swept over him. His mind's eye could see clearly the lifeless form of the beautiful young native woman on the beach, and he could still hear the screams of the blonde woman in the nun's habit as she looked back at Konovalov on the opposite side of the river. The childhood stories of Rusalka filled his mind with fear as he panicked. If the skiff sank, he would go under the freezing waves, down to the murky depths of Rusalka's reign for all eternity. He vomited in a dry heave. He bent over and cupping both hands, began to scoop water out as fast as he could toss it over the side and back into the inlet.

Konovalov's heart pounded hard in his chest, and his breath was so ragged that the thought crossed his mind that he would not perish of drowning, but of a heart attack. He paused a moment and glanced up to gauge how far Kasilof was from his skiff. He was shocked to see an unfamiliar vessel gliding at full sail far beyond the delta of Kasilof. He realized it was a Spanish galleon, and it was almost out of sight.

Konovalov paused a long moment, staring at the Spanish vessel as it shrank in size on the horizon. Then, an idea washed over him like the cold waves about him in the inlet. The beautiful nun, Sophia was escaping. How did she get word to the Spanish to rescue her? Relief and frustration swept over Konovalov. He was frustrated that the witness to his crime had escaped to Spain and forever beyond his reach. At the same time, it was like a huge stone lifted from his back.

Sophia was not dead. Since the drowning of the native woman, Konovalov had tried to drown his own guilt and fear in vodka. He had hidden in the fort trying to forget that somewhere out there Sophia was waiting for revenge.

Konovalov scoffed and chided himself as he realized who was behind the ghost of Kenay. Sophia had taken advantage of the Russian's fear of Rusalka and tormented them in their guilty minds for Anna's death by drowning in the river. There was no real Rusalka. It was all just a fairy tale told to frighten children and men who mistreated women. Nothing more. As the weight of fear and guilt slipped from Konovalov's mind over Sophia, he returned to his present predicament. His skiff was in danger of going under and dumping him in the cold inlet water.

Konovalov thought of his sailing skills. He glanced at the eastern shore. He tried to assess the distance and the speed of the wind pushing the sails and driving the skiff forward. The wind was pushing him away from the beaches of Kasilof and out across the inlet. He squinted towards the western shore of the inlet. It was still too far to land safely. He couldn't keep the water out of the skiff fast enough to reach the opposite shore. Just as death by drowning loomed again in his mind, Konovalov caught sight of hope. In the distance, he spotted the sails of the St. George.

Zaikov was returning from Tyonek. Konovalov cried and adjusted the sails. The skiff burst forward over the waves so fast towards the St. George that the water slowed its splashing into the skiff. He began scooping the liquid out of the boat with all the effort he could muster.

AS THE SPANISH SHIP PULLED ANCHOR and Nicholas stood on the deck, he heard a yell. The Spaniards were pointing westward. Nicholas squinted. He recognized the St. George's sails across the fifty miles of inlet water between them. He guessed that Zaikov was returning to the fort on the Kenay. He doubted that Zaikov would have heard of the Denaina attack on the fort, but knew that the Captain would soon find out. He wondered if Acts Quickly was alive. He had never seen actual combat himself and contemplated briefly what it felt like to kill a man. Nicholas was startled out of his reverie by a bump on his shoulder.

It was Salvadore. "Look, take the spyglass and look. There. Off the eastern shore." Salvadore thrust the glass into Nicholas' hand. Nicholas raised the glass and scanned the shore. It took him a long moment to find what the Spaniard was remarking on. Nicholas wasn't sure what he saw until he held his breath and steadied himself against the rocking of the ship on the tide. A tiny white dot. He stared questioningly at Salvadore.

The Spaniard laughed, flashing brilliant white even teeth. "It is the sail of the skiff. The skiff we filled with rifles for the Denaina. Someone has escaped."

Nicholas peered back through the glass. He could make out the tiny white sail. He studied it until the Spanish vessel raised sail and began to glide swiftly and capably from the shores, farther from the Russian vessel on the far shore.

Nicholas stood on the deck as he had weeks earlier during his arrival on the St. George. How innocent he had been when he sailed into the inlet. He hadn't expected the terror that awaited him at the redoubt. He had not expected to meet an impressive native man of his own age whose path in life was the same, and yet so different. The haunting of the Kenai was now over. The evil deeds done by the Russians were being judged. War had been waged on the beautiful bluffs. The fort was no longer visible behind a cloud of smoke. Nicholas turned his face towards the west, hoping to catch a last glimpse of the St. George returning from Tyonek on the west side of the inlet, but the Spanish galleon was racing over the ocean too fast, and the scenery streamed by. Above the waters, the mighty mountain loomed.

A puff of steam rose from the peak. "Even the mountain is burning," thought Nicholas. And he turned his thoughts to Spain.

THIRTEEN

Acts Quickly hurriedly and carefully carried his father down the trail and back to the chief's home in the native village. With each step the chief's body grew heavier, and Acts Quickly fought off a mounting terror that his father had died on the way home. When Acts Quickly finally laid his father on the kitchen table, his mother leaned over the chief and listened to the wounded man's breathing.

"He's alive. He's still breathing," she exclaimed softly, with a look of immense relief at her son.

Acts Quickly helped his mother clean and dress the wound in his father's shoulder. Then, the son carried his father to the bed and settled him comfortably to rest. Acts Quickly's mother settled down near the bed and began an anxious and attentive vigil over her husband.

"Here." Acts Quickly took the pouch with his sister's gold cross in it and handed it to his mother.

She took it and opened it, slowly pulling out the cross and

gripping it tightly in her hand. She spoke in a hoarse whisper, "I feel like she is watching over us. I feel her presence here now."

The woman glanced from her husband to her son with tears welling up in her eyes. "I feel like she is at peace. She is near and yet, everything is restored. It will be okay."

Acts Quickly nodded. "I must go, Mother. The villagers need me to help them, and we need to bring the other wounded men home," Acts Quickly explained.

His mother nodded in approval.

Acts Quickly returned to the fort. The sun was beginning to set. The groans of wounded men and the stench of death and despair from the dying hung over the fort like a fog. Acts Quickly called together the Denaina men who were still able-bodied and discussed with them what needed to be done. The wounded Denaina warriors were taken back to the village to be cared for by their families. There were a handful of wounded Russians still alive. Acts Quickly had them put in the men's barracks and made them as comfortable as possible, as they would stay there until he could consult with the village elders , about what was to be done with the remaining Russians.

When the wounded had been cared for, their injuries dressed at the village and their bodies made comfortable to begin the healing process, Acts Quickly gathered the village elders and held a short meeting with them. It was decided that the dead of both the Russians and the Denaina would be burned on separate massive funeral pyres. The elderly, women, and older children would help by gathering wood while the surviving men of the village started the gruesome and sorrowful task of caring for the bodies of those who had bravely fought and died. The bodies of Denaina warriors were respectfully carried to the expanse of river bar near the village. Driftwood from large trees that had fallen into the river and been swept down to rest on the sand bars were easily gathered and now provided fuel for the massive fires that would burn the dead, so that their spirits would be released to walk on into the next world.

The dead Russians were hastily brought to the center of the redoubt yard, where wood from the fort walls had been torn down and to burn their remains. The wounded Russians lay unattended in the bunkhouses, and would have to wait until the dead were taken care of the next day. The elders needed time to decide what to do with those Russians who remained alive.

GREGORI KONOVALOV SAT ON THE DECK of St. George the Victorious, unable to catch his breath or speak for long minutes. The tiny skiff had carried him across the inlet to meet the ship, where the crew had hoisted the lone sailor up and onto the decks. The skiff was not tied up, and as it caught the wind in its tiny sails it veered off towards the far reaches of the inlet, until it was out of sight. Konovalov wanted to cry with relief, but his teeth began to chatter from the icy wind so violently that he couldn't speak. He sat with his knees drawn up to his chest and looked pitifully up at the crew. He could tell by the look on Captain Zaikov's face that the man was furious with him. Zaikov scowled at the pathetic sight of the garrison commander huddling on his ship's deck in soaked clothes.

Konovalov was shivering uncontrollably and whimpering. "The man needs dry clothes and something to warm him up or he will die before our eyes," Father Iosaf warned Zaikov, as he leaned over to inspect Konovalov.

"Take him to Balushin's quarters and lock him there. Then report to me in my quarters," Zaikov barked. The priest followed the two crew members who stepped forward to pick up Konovalov and take him below the deck.

After making sure the fort commander Konovalov was made comfortable, the priest and the first mate returned to Zaikov with a report. "He is resting in blankets with Balushin watching over him. He spoke a few words, sir, as we carried him below deck. He said the natives attacked the fort and that he alone escaped. He said he was trying to sail to Kasilof and get the men there to return to the redoubt with him and fight off the natives to rescue the men at the fort."

Zaikov slammed his fist on the table.

He roared, "I knew this would happen. The fool. I warned him that using such heavy-handed tactics in the practice trade and slavery of the natives would result in violent attacks on our redoubts in Kodiak and on the Aleutian Islands."

He turned back to the first mate. "Did he say how many men are dead? Did he stay around long enough to find out how bad the fighting was, or did he run like a coward when the first shot rang out?"

The first mate shook his head, "The man is in terrible shape. Perhaps you can get the full story out of him in a little while when he has recovered and warmed up." Zaikov's anger increased.

Father Iosaf cleared his throat and spoke calmly, "A spoon full of honey attracts more flies than a spoon full of vinegar."

Zaikov replied, "You mean a shot glass of vodka loosens lips of a drunk."

The priest nodded, "The vodka will warm him up, and he will recover remarkably fast and tell you what you need to know. After all, you need to figure out if it is safe to continue back to the Kenay."

Zaikov sighed and crossed the room to a cupboard. He drew out a bottle of vodka and handed it to the first mate. "Give him one shot. Then bring him to me. And tell the crew to steer toward Kasilof. We go to the safety of the redoubt there first."

THE NIGHT CREPT ACROSS YAGHANEN. The sun dropped sadly behind the shoulders of the sullen white capped mountains to the west of the inlet. The foothills to the east transformed with a purple tint in the dying light, before darkening until they could not be seen any longer. A great conspiracy of ravens gathered above the fort. The only sound in the gloom was the swoosh of their black wings as they swooped over the bodies and landed on the walls for a moment, before taking wing again.

Acts Quickly and several men accompanied the village elder to the spring behind the village. Several buckets of water were drawn as the men hastily returned to the village. The Denaina elder led the way through the village to each house with the men carrying the buckets behind him. As the elder approached a door, he began to sing a song in Denaina. Acts Quickly knew the song was from ancient times, and that it was given to the Denaina to sing by the Helper Spirit. Each door opened and the villager held out a cup. Acts Quickly ladled a cup of water from the bucket and helped to set the cup beside the doorway. The practice of placing a cup of water in the corner of the doorway of a house was the tradition of keeping the spirits of the dead from entering the house, a tradition practiced since time immemorial. The procession ended at Acts Quickly's home. He thanked the men and the elder. The men assured him that they would see the elder safely home before returning to their own. Acts Quickly closed the door and took his place by his mother in her vigil by his father's side.

In the early dawn, the chief stirred. He winced and groaned. Acts Quickly woke and rushed to his side where his mother had remained awake.

"Father." Acts Quickly's voice was thick with emotion and relief.

His father opened his eyes for a moment and gazed dully at his wife and son. He sighed deeply and closed his eyes again.

"He needs to rest more," Act's Quickly's mother murmured in assurance. Her mouth smiled and the tautness loosened in her face. After a long moment of silence, as the mother and son listened to the chief's steady breathing, she put her hand on her Acts Quickly's arm.

She spoke quietly, "You are a good son, and you are a good chief."

A shadow of fear crossed Acts Quickly's face. He stared at his mother before he grasped the meaning of her words.

She continued, "When the men needed a chief today, you stood up and led them. When our villagers needed a leader, you were there. I don't mean that your father will die tonight, or that you will now have to take over his position and be our chief. I mean that he will heal, and will have you as a chief beside him. He will need your help and will rely on your strength. I am proud of you, Son." She smiled at Acts Quickly.

He grinned back, his heart swelling at the words of his mother.

THE CREW OF THE ST. GEORGE BUSIED THEMSELVES with the new orders to steer the vessel towards the Kasilof Redoubt. The first mate returned hastily to the Captain's quarters, followed by a stumbling Konovalov who was dragged by two burly crew members, one holding each arm. Konovalov was dumped roughly into a chair at the table before Zaikov as the first mate set the bottle of vodka and a small glass on the table in front of him. Zaikov stared with cold eyes at the man before him. Father Iosaf sat unobtrusively at the far end of the table, stroking his beard thoughtfully as he observed the two company men in front of him. Konovalov licked his lips nervously as his eyes darted between the vodka bottle and the floor. Zaikov scoffed in disgust.

"Tell me everything." He pulled the bottle closer and poured a shot in the glass as he waited for Konovalov to answer him.

"The young officer who came with you, well, he disappeared. He was gone in the morning and Demidov and Vasilov were going to go to the village with a group of armed men as a search party."

Konovalov stuttered over the words gushing from his mouth.

"But before they could put together a search party, the natives showed up at the fort. They brought a bunch of furs to trade, so the officers let them inside the gate." Zaikov slid the glass across the table. Konovalov lifted the vodka to his lips eagerly and finished the shot in a gulp. He set the glass down. The burning liquid cleared his head. He began to carefully relate all the events that occurred at the redoubt after Zaikov's departure.

He complained a little that he had suffered without Balushin's comforting help and had to instead rely on Igor. He was bitter that when he needed him the most, Igor had not been able to enter the officers' quarters under Demidov's and Vasilov's orders. Despite lying in his bed under the auspices of being too ill to work, Konovalov had heard all that had been going on in the fort. The skiff, the bear and the gift of beluga meat were all recounted. He was careful with the details of the battle. Somewhere the natives had gotten rifles.

The Spanish, in the commander's suspicions, had most likely provided the rifles in exchange for furs and supplies. As Zaikov listened attentively, his face was impassive. The Captain carefully scrutinized Konovalov's face for any hints of falsehood. Konovalov continued his account, lamenting sadly the death of Igor as well as the officers, Demidov and Vasilov, whom Zaikov had left in charge at the fort. Konovalov recalled in an admirable way that as the last Russian standing, he had valiantly fought his way out of the fort and barely escaped to the skiff. As the last Russian alive, he knew he must get to Kasilof and warn the company men there that the natives were rebelling. The vodka had fully warmed Konovalov.

He drew himself up and held up his chin. It was due to his superior sailing skills that allowed him to sail across the inlet, board the St. George, and now sit before the Captain to enlighten him about the horrific tragedy he had endured and singularly survived at the fort. The fort which had been abandoned without enough men to work or defend the redoubt against the natives who had taken advantage of the weak defense, all because Zaikov wanted to go to Tyonek and with extra men.

After all, if Zaikov had known anything about the company and its struggle to survive and thrive in Alaska, he would have known that the native people would attack the Russians unjustly from time to time, and would not have allowed the fort to be shorthanded on men to defend it. Zaikov stared at Konovalov, in disbelief that the commander could so easily change from a sick man with an ulcer. To a simpering half drowned escapee, and finally to the arrogant man who was accusing him of causing the war at the fort.

As fury rose in the Captain, the priest stood up and held his hand up in protest as he addressed him. "Captain Zaikov, do not believe him. Don't give his words any credence. He is a liar and a coward."

Konovalov started. He cut short a curse as he remembered he was facing a priest. He began to protest. "Why do you say such things, Father Iosaf? They are not true. You do not know me," Konovalov's voice began to whine.

"I have suffered at that fort for years. Neither of you know how hard it was to build that fort and stay there all winter. I had to make sure two hundred men were fed, taken care of and protected. I had to build the St. Nicholas Redoubt because the Lebedev company was not welcome in Kasilof. I had to start the trade with the natives there, in spite of the Kasilof Redoubt always trying to steal our trade. And what did either of you do? You come from Russia where you are warm and have all the nice food you can eat and live in nice houses. You come here and judge me." Konovalov thumped his chest.

He continued, "I had to do all the work. I did. There would be no St. Nicholas Redoubt if it weren't for me and all that I have done. I don't deserve to be called a liar and a coward for the work I have done. I don't. I will not be talked to that way."

He jabbed his finger at the priest and Captain. "I will report you two to the company. I will. You wait and see. I will tell them how you both conspired against me."

Konovalov stood up and faced the priest. "You. What did you do in the village the day before you sailed to Tyonek? Did you know the natives were going to attack? You talked to the chief. Did you tell him to attack?" Konovalov's face turned deep purple with indignation as he turned towards Zaikov.

"And you. You took my men to Tyonek. We couldn't defend ourselves because we didn't have enough men. Both of you are in on this war together. I will tell the company that you caused the war. I see you did not count on me being such a formidable man. But I survived the attack. I will tell the company." As Konovalov finished, he stood with his chest heaving and his eyes blazing. He scooped up the bottle and drank a long deep drag of vodka. He wiped his mouth on the sleeve of his shirt as he glared at the other men as if daring them to defy his accusations.

"I don't believe a word he says about the battle. Don't listen to him, Captain. Don't believe him." Father Iosaf returned evenly and firmly. Zaikov looked at the two men with narrowed eyes and a dangerous look on his face.

"Liar?" Konovalov retorted. "You priests are the liars."

"Watch your mouth," barked Zaikov.

Father Iosaf went on calmly, "I say you are a liar because you lied to Father Juvenal." Konovalov sputtered, "About what?"

"About the woman," the priest answered. There was silence.

In a desperate effort to keep face, Konovalov asked, "Wha . . . Wha . . . What woman?" The garrison commander's face was pale, and he trembled as he fell back into his chair.

"The native woman who drowned because of you," Father Iosaf

spoke in a quiet voice.

"You can't prove anything. You are the one who is lying now." Konovalov argued.

Father Iosaf reached inside his robes and drew out a tattered leather-bound journal. "It is all in here, Konovalov."

The priest turned to Zaikov, "Captain, I insist that Konovalov and Balushin be arrested and returned to Russia to stand trial for murder, slavery, and inciting a war with the native peoples here after interfering with the Orthodox missions to convert them."

He paused a moment and continued slowly and surely. "This is Father Juvenal's journal. He left it for me in Tyonek. The old native couple gave it to me when we were there. Father Juvenal left Fort Kenay for Tyonek because he feared for his life and the life of the woman who was traveling with him as his nun."

"He hid her from you, Konovalov. He realized that you would never allow a true Orthodox mission to be built and thrive at Kenay. He knew you were causing trouble with the natives through sex slavery, the taking of concubines from the native women, and threats of violence when they tried to trade the furs honestly." The priest held the journal open for the men to see the pages of neat Cyrillic script.

"It's all in here. The Denaina chief's daughter converted under Father Juvenal. She wanted to become a nun. She constantly accompanied the nun, Sister Sophia, Father Juvenal brought with him, a good and holy woman."

The priest pointed at Konovalov. "You and Balushin tried to rape the women. They went into the river and drowned. Or so you thought. The nun survived and hid. She told Father Juvenal everything. There was no ghost. There was no Rasulka. There was only your guilty conscience and a nun who survived the evil you intended for her."

Konovalov fainted and fell from his chair with a heavy thud on the floor.

"Take him back and lock him up with Balushin." Zaikov ordered. When the crew had left with the drunken commander, the Captain turned to the priest.

"If what you say is true, this is a very serious charge." Father Iosaf handed him the journal. "Read it. It is all in there. Father Juvenal kept a careful account of everything that Konovalov and the men at the fort did. The injustices and the evils that Konovalov and his men did bring about the war. It is a small wonder that the natives wanted to drive out the Russians and destroy the fort."

Zaikov took the journal from the priest and sat down again at the table. He called for a light and began reading. Father Iosaf sat still in his chair, turning beads in his hand as he prayed silently.

After several hours, Zaikov closed the book and rubbed his eyes wearily. "We sail to Russia. We take Konovalov and Balushin with us to stand trial."

"What about the fort? Should we not go to the fort first and see if anyone is still there? What about rebuilding it and holding it through the winter?" Father Iosaf questioned the Captain.

Zaikov shook his head. "Konovalov said there were no survivors. We will drop the men we took from Redoubt Nicholas with us to Tyonek off at Kasilof tomorrow. We will warn the company men there to be prepared for war at Kasilof. There is no need for us to go to Kenay and fight with the natives. We are not ready for a battle ourselves. If there are men still alive there at Fort Kenay, Konovalov will have to answer for them, since he told us no one survived. We will take Balushin and Konovalov back to Russia, and let the company decide what to do with them and with the fort. I want to sail before the weather changes." The priest nodded in agreement.

Zaikov sat still for several minutes as he pondered what he had read in the journal. He turned towards Father Iosaf.

"Father Juvenal writes that the nun Sister Sophia who he

traveled with was not a real nun. She was Princess Sophia. The woman in white who stood on the beach screaming and haunting the fort was the rightful heir to the throne of the Russian empire. She must be the reason young Nicholas was sent here." He looked at the priest in search of an answer.

Father Iosaf chuckled softly. He rose stiffly and strode towards the door. He turned back with one hand on the knob to address the Captain in amusement. "We both know who was safely escaping this godforsaken country on that Spanish galleon, Captain. I think Nicholas did what he was sent here to do. May God bless him and our Tsarina."

He bowed his head as he exited the Captain's quarters, "Good night, Captain Zaikov."

FOURTEEN

Ancestors, accept my gift. Look upon me kindly and bless my hunting. I am Qadanalchen, son of the Qeshqa, Chief of the Denaina. Qadanalchen, known as Acts Quickly, laid the offering of dried fish on the ground. The young man straightened and looked at his surroundings. Acts Quickly was alone.

Acts Quickly called to his mind the time after his vision quest when over a year ago, he had stood in the clearing waiting for his father, his cousins Spear and Last Waters, and the village elder to arrive upriver from their village to meet him and bring him home. Now, Acts Quickly's son had finished his vision quest and was ready to return home, a changed young man. The quest had begun several days before in an area between two mountain peaks a few miles from the clearing. His camp was in scrub willows near a spring running from the rocky slope. The days had been bright and sunny. and the nights illuminated by stars.

On the last night, it was the Dreamer himself that came to Acts Quickly. He came across the hillside at sunset and approached without speaking. Dreamer watched the sunset with Acts Quickly before turning to him and motioning. Acts Quickly followed him to a rock outcropping above his camp.

The entire valley stretched out below. A star burned out across the sky. Despite the descending darkness, Acts Quickly could see every kind of animal that walked on four legs, along with every kind of bird with wings arriving for the first time into the valley. He smiled as he listened to the endless chorus of voices as the spirits of each creature chattered and sang songs. Acts Quickly could not contain a chuckle as he watched a pair of wolf pups chase each other's tails. Acts Quickly glanced at Dreamer, the Raven Spirit, who formed the world and its beings. To his surprise, four others stood around Acts Quickly, like sentinels looking on. Acts Quickly recognized each of the visitors. There was the Prophet, the Sky Reader, the Shaman, and the Physician. The four stood silently gazing at the valley. Acts Quickly turned his attention there as well. He saw small figures pouring across the slopes. He heard voices and his heart swelled. It was the Campfire People. These were the ancestors. Acts Quickly noticed they showed great respect to every life form in the valley as they ran and jumped across the slopes, speaking to each spirit in kind and singing songs. Acts Quickly felt a timeless belonging and great peace.

Prophet spoke, "The time of the Campfire People is over. The strangers have come. The Russians are insulting the spirits of all living things. They don't listen. They don't respect."

"Will they leave again?" Acts Quickly questioned anxiously. To his deepest dismay, Prophet shook his head. There was a long silence as the starlight faded and the darkness of the night overtook the valley and the vision of the Campfire People faded.

Prophet spoke again,. "The Kahtnuht'ana will go to war."

It was then that Sky Reader murmured, "On the morning of the war, the sky will be red, like blood. That is the color of the morning sky when the Kahtnuht'ana warriors will attack the white men in their fort."

The Physician added, "Many men will die, both white men and Kahtnuht'ana. But you will live. You will not be harmed."

Prophet continued, "After the war, the Russians will return. They will try to end the Kahtnuht'ana by spreading a sickness. The Russians know that this evil sickness is new to the Kahtnuht'ana and that they will die of the disease because their bodies don't know the evil. But good Russian priests will bring medicine that will save the people from the sickness so that the Kahtnuht'ana will survive. Things will change. Many white people will come and live on the land. The spirits of the land and the ancestors will be forgotten by most ,but not all. The Kahtnuht'ana will remain. You will lead the people and tell them that the ways remain."

Shaman came to Acts Quickly and put his hands on him. He sang a song over the boy. Acts Quickly never forgot the song. Shaman whispered in the young man's ear. Acts Quickly never forgot the words. He waited respectfully as the Dreamer and his companions stood a while longer, before disappearing into the inky blackness of the night.

Acts Quickly looked around. He found he was sitting in his camp again. The stars were bright above him. Acts Quickly sat all night singing the song taught to him by the Shaman. It was on the following night that the Helper spirit came to the chief's son. The Spirit came from far below and made its way up the valley steadily until it stood at the edge of Acts Quickly's camp. There the Helper waited until Acts Quickly offered it some food and invited it into his camp. The Spirit was pleased with the invitation and joined Acts Quickly. What happened that night, Acts Quickly kept to himself according to the Helper's wishes. He never told what power the Helper had given him.

His sister had asked Acts Quickly about his vision quest once.

She had noticed the change in her brother immediately and was curious about what he experienced that night. She was curious about the Helper and Dreamer and the other Spirits. Acts Quickly had felt reluctant to tell her. Ada was now Anna, a baptized Orthodox Christian. He had respected her choice and the power of the priest, but he was hesitant to follow her just yet. Now, following the war at the redoubt, Acts Quickly knew it was time to join his sister's way. He was at peace with her death. Her words at the water's edge when Acts Quickly was an instant away from pulling the pistol trigger to shoot Konovalov had stopped the revenge killing and transformed everything. Now, Acts Quickly realized the might of the power of forgiveness and why his sister had been baptized.

Acts Quickly put the pouch on the ground as a final offering to the Spirits, the Ancestors, and the land. He prayed for his father, who still lay wounded in his home and for his mother who wept silently as she cared for her husband. The mourning cries of the Denaina women and children for their father, husband, son or brother lost in the battle echoed in his ears. The crackling of the funeral pyres of the fallen Kahtnuht'ana warriors reverberated in his mind. Acts Quickly slowly exhaled. He released all their cries and loss to the wind.

Konovalov and the surviving Russians had fled after the war. Acts Quickly knew the invaders would return in greater numbers. He stood still, listening. Acts Quickly thought of Dreamer, Prophet Shaman, Sky Reader, and Physician. The Prophet had seen and foretold that the Denaina would fight, and that many more would die when new invaders would come. There would be a great sickness of smallpox which would cause many deaths, and the Russian priests would bring a cure of vaccines to heal the sick.

The Denaina would survive. "I forgive them, Anna. I set you free."

Acts Quickly breathed and turned toward home. The ghosts of the Kenai no longer wailed on the wind. He felt peace fill his heart.

GROWING UP ON THE BANKS OF the Copper River, Aurora Hardy read voraciously. Without electricity or modern conveniences, while homeschooling, Aurora entertained herself by reading. Aurora also wrote, keeping a journal, making a 'newspaper' and recording the beauty of the land in poetry. She was published several times in Howard Rock's Alaska Native newspaper, The Tundra Times.

In 1986, Aurora was the first Native woman to graduate from the University of Montana School of Forestry. Her work demanded technical and scientific report writing, but Aurora always dreamed of writing her own stories. In 2007, she published *Terror at Black Rapids*, about a terrorist attack on the Alaska Pipeline. As she worked, raised children and became a grandparent, Aurora wrote stories and poems. The City of Kenai chose one of her poems about a dog walking the beach in a contest in 2019.

Aurora has survived racism, mission boarding school, 1964 earthquake and tsunami, poverty, and many other challenges facing Native women. Her imagination helped her through many adversities. In dreaming stories and poems, she found strength and courage to hope for a better future. Aurora is dedicated to inspire reading to young Alaskans.

www.ingramcontent.com/pod-product-compliance
Lightning Source LLC
Chambersburg PA
CBHW011519100726
47899CB00010BD/3430